SHOWTIME

Tracker was greeted by a burst of gunfire from his own MAC-11. Scared but grinning, the killer walked down the long hallway brandishing Natty's machine pistols. Instead of ducking, Natty jumped straight in the air and executed a flying snap kick that shattered the lone light bulb illuminating the hallway. Now the killer fired blindly. Natty laughed and dodged the bullets. The killer had weapons, but couldn't see.

Tracker could see everything. . .

D1234711

TRACKER

RON STILLMAN

CHARTER/DIAMOND BOOKS, NEW YORK

TRACKER

A Charter/Diamond Book / published by arrangement with
the author

PRINTING HISTORY
Charter/Diamond edition / September 1990

ISBN: 1-55773-384-8

Charter/Diamond Books are published by The Berkley Publishing
Group, 200 Madison Avenue, New York, New York 10016.
The name ''CHARTER/DIAMOND'' and its logo are trademarks
belonging to Charter Communications, Inc.

PRINTED IN THE UNITED STATES OF AMERICA

10 9 8 7 6 5 4 3 2 1

1.

Please Bear with Him

THE SCIENTISTS LABELED him *Ursus Arctos*, whereas his inland cousin, the grizzly, was called *Ursus Horribilis*. This old boy, however, dwarfed all but the largest grizzlies. A resident of Afognak Island southwest of Anchorage for all of his seven years, he now stood eight and a half feet tall on his hind legs and weighed 1,257 pounds. Due to the longer growing season, rich soil, and a diet much richer in salmon, the Alaskan brown bear frequently grows larger than the grizzly. Both have a dish-faced, hump-backed look and very long, non-retractable claws, and a disposition somewhere between that of Don Rickles and the late Ayatollah Cockamamie.

Most old-timers would refer to this big bear as a Kodiak, a label many give to the Alaskan brown bear, but technically that bear is only found on neighboring Kodiak Island. This experiment, however, was taking place on the Kodiak National Wildlife Refuge that included both Kodiak and Afognak Islands.

The ferocious bear moved easily through a claustrophobic devil's club and alders thicket, halting at the edge of a salmon-choked stream. Moonlight reflected off fast-moving ripples as the bruin stood on his massive hind legs, nose testing the wind.

A video camera with a night-vision lens panned slowly with the bear's movements twelve feet below the camera's tree-limb mount. The bear smelled a human downwind, but the man had known of the bear's presence for ten minutes.

Major Nathaniel Hawthorne Tracker looked at the device on his left wrist. It was another of his inventions, and he was now proving its value to his lifeblood, home, and womb . . . the United States Air Force. The device on Tracker's arm resembled a large wristwatch and had a small computer screen with a current readout of 80 ESE-S, which meant that the warm-blooded object was eighty meters to the east-southeast and was stationary. Earlier, the device had given the speed and direction of travel of the bear.

The "Tracker System" was developed by Natty for use by pilots or others stranded behind enemy lines to evade capture and escape. One of the military's top computer experts, Tracker was also a top radar officer.

Loving adrenaline highs even more than gadgets, he had left his radar job and opted for flight school. He had been a jet jockey at Elmendorf Air Force Base just north of Anchorage for a year when he developed the Tracker System during his spare time. Piloting an F-15C Eagle, Natty flew the narrow corridor between the United States and the Soviet Union over the Bering Strait. As a member of the 21st Tactical Fighter Wing, he had flown a number of missions alongside Soviet Tupolev TU-126 Moss, TU-95 Bear, and other Russian aircraft. He and the Soviet pilots often waved at each other, took photographs, or jokingly made indecent gestures. His nights had been spent inventing tracking devices utilizing radar, infrared, and sonar technologies.

To prove the value of his system, Tracker had convinced Air Force and other government officials to travel to Alaska for a daring demonstration. Working with officials from the Alaska Wildlife Division, they had implanted twenty video cameras with night-vision lenses along a selected stream on Afognak Island, which was noted for its large brown bear population and the bears' nocturnal activities. Air Force personnel and observers from the CIA, the Defense Intelligence Agency, FBI, and USSOCOM (US Special Operations Command) from Macdill Air Force Base, Florida, were sequestered in observation trailers near the head of the stream. Tracker, meanwhile was traversing the bruin-infested waterway, unarmed and after midnight, for its entire length, utilizing the Tracker System to warn him of the deadly animals.

On his right wrist, Natty watched a miniaturized video screen, another of his inventions, that showed the dark woods ahead of him with daylight quality. This was a variation of the state-of-the-art system under development for jet aircraft by Martin Marietta, called the Lantern System, combined with the older Starlight technology used by the US Army on its Starlight scopes that magnify available star and moonlight for night visibility. The miniature video screen received a broadcast from a miniature video camera that was built into Natty's flight helmet.

The Tracker System utilized a sonar program and a heat-sensing device that was so sensitive Natty had picked up a reading on fresh puddles of urine and piles of dung from animals while testing the system. The sonar and body heat readings were sent to and deciphered by a microchip developed by Natty and a civilian buddy working in Silicon Valley.

When Tracker got a reading indicating he was forty meters from the large bear, he started inland to work around it. He pushed a button on the side of the Tracker System and instantly got a reading on a sow and two cubs that were sixty yards off and moving away from him. Thus far, the tall fighter pilot had detected and avoided over fifty bears and had just two miles to go to reach the base area at the source of the stream.

His paternal grandfather had been an Assiniboin Sioux Indian, and his paternal grandmother was black. His maternal grandmother was Tonto Apache, and his maternal grandfather had been a blond-haired, blue-eyed Norwegian. Nat Tracker ended up with short wavy black hair, a very dark complexion, and powder-blue eyes. Strikingly handsome, he stood six-feet-four and would be considered slender. A renowned wide-receiver at the Air Force Academy, his tiny waist yielded to a washboard stomach and an extremely muscular chest and shoulders. He was born with long, flexible runner's legs. These were developed to their fullest by the grueling discipline required to achieve a second degree black belt in Song Moo Kwan Tae Kwon Do, a Korean form of karate noted for its powerful and intricate kicking techniques.

Growing up on a ranch in the West, Natty had learned from his father and his grandparents how to look at a track and know it was a coyote's and not a dog's because the two middle toes were longer. He could look at the track of a mountain lion and determine if it was a male or female by the roundness and space between the toe pads. Natty's granddad on his father's side passed on the family tradition to the eager youngster by teaching him the ancient techniques of tracking. The hours of study gave the boy an inquisitive and comprehensive mind. He learned to follow the trail of man or beast and learned like all the great Native American trackers to read the mind of his quarry by reading the trail signs. By the age of twelve, Natty could just about track a trout upstream or follow a snake over a flat rock in dry weather. He had earned the family name. He had also developed a love for James Bond novels and movies and was especially fond of the gadgets in them.

A boy of much curiosity and self-discipline, Nat Tracker was an outstanding scholar/athlete throughout his schooling. He easily won an appointment to the US Air Force Academy, south of his home in Colorado Springs, and he graduated with honors. He had first developed an interest in Tae Kwon Do at the age of ten when his father, a sergeant major in the US Army, was stationed as an advisor to the White Horse Division of the South Korean Army. His father had become a computer expert when they were still called "electronic brains."

Referring to it as "electronic heroin," Natty's dad had to force him to limit his hours in video arcades. In high school, Natty spent hours in front of munching Pac Man monsters, slithering electronic centipedes, and other computerized demons. He was fascinated with the patterns set up by the machines' computer chips, and he was forever challenged to figure them out.

Tracker looked at his left wrist again as alarm registered on his face. The big bear had caught his scent and was now headed toward him at a high rate of speed.

Lieutenant Commander Jake Mortimer, representing SOCOM, had just poured a hot cup of coffee and now looked at his diver's watch. It was a few hours before dawn. He looked at the video monitors and alerted the others in the observation trailers. They all watched with eyes and mouths opened wide.

Tracker knew he had to act—and act fast. An Alaskan brown bear could outrun a race horse on flat ground and could snap a moose's spine with one bite or decapitate a man with one swipe of a mighty forepaw. A very large, obstinate bear was headed his way with one of those goals in mind. Many bears scenting a man would have gone away, but bears are like people; there are peace-lovers, bullies, all sorts. This one didn't like humans and had decided to prove it. Natty looked for a nearby tree to climb but saw only stunted alders.

When attacked by a bear one has four choices: (1) Shoot it; (2) Climb a thin but strong tree; (3) Lie on one's stomach and play dead with one's fingers interlocked behind one's neck; or (4) Try to make a run for your pack-mule and give it a long lingering smooch; in other words, you can kiss your ass good-bye. Tracker thought all this in a millisecond with a very strong consideration for option number four.

In one of the observation trailers, a beautiful green-eyed bombshell with waist-length auburn hair watched man and bear on two screens. Her pouting lips opened in horror, and Dr. Fancy Bird worried about the fate of the tall pilot she had been fantasizing about. His powder-blue eyes and knowing smile had penetrated her and had traveled through her shapely body, causing a tingling in her loins.

Fancy had a doctorate in political science from Georgetown and was a GS-13 with the CIA at Langley, Virginia. She had spent two years in Teheran, one in El Salvador, and had a bullet scar from Nicaragua. She'd never been flustered by any man before, but when Tracker's baby-blue eyes put her green ones on radar lock-on, she became weak-kneed and tongue-tied. Fancy sensed that this man would allow her her independence but could protect her from any danger. Sensing this, she relaxed a little as she watched the drama unfold on the video monitors.

Pushing the tiny button on the side of his tracking device, Natty got another reading on the sow and cubs and took off in her direction at a dead run. The huge bear was closing as Nat yelled at the far-off female bear.

"Hey, Mama! I'm comin' at you, and I'm gonna beat the shit out of your babies!"

Natty grinned as he looked down at his Tracker System and saw that the now-angry sow, certain that her cubs were in danger, was bearing down on him at full speed. She was forty-five yards off and moving like a freight train, and the noise of her crashing through the alders reverberated through the stillness of the chilly Alaskan night. Close behind him, the big male continued thrashing through the underbrush.

Looking at the miniature video screen on his right wrist, Natty dived under a low branch on the right of the trail and scrambled into a thicket on hands and knees for ten yards. He froze in place and listened as the gargantuan bear and angry sow rammed into each other in a biting, clawing battle royal. Quickly and carefully, Tracker crawled away and headed back toward his destination.

Fancy's heart pounded as she looked at the center monitor and watched the handsome pilot wink at the last camera as he passed beneath it.

It wasn't long before Tracker arrived at the base camp where he was greeted by a cheering throng of government experts. His eyes locked with Fancy's, and again her heart raced as he walked over to her.

"I'm very impressed," she said coyly.

"Thank you, Doctor Bird," he said.

"Fancy, please, Major Tracker," she replied. "I thought that bear was going to eat you."

"No problem," he replied with a warm smile. "And you can call me Natty. Thanks for your concern. Ah . . . is Fancy Bird your given name?"

She blushed. "Yes, it is."

"I could sure use a drink, and I'd love to find out how you got your name," Natty offered.

"I'd love it, Natty." Fancy let a small giggle escape. "You like my name, huh?"

The tall pilot took her gently by the arm and guided her toward one of the trailers.

He grinned, "That and your plumage. This could be a deep subject, but I'd love to plunge into it."

"I bet," she said demurely.

2.

Something to Kick About

THREE DAYS PASSED and Natty Tracker's invention was now owned by the US Government. Fancy had an early flight to Dulles Airport near Washington and awakened shortly after daybreak.

Looking above the bed in her motel room, she started giggling. Soon she held her arms over her midsection, laughing hysterically. Taped to the ceiling above her were several condoms blown up like balloons.

Natty had written on them in her lipstick: "Loved our time together. See you when I go back East. Love, Tracker."

Still nude and laughing, the shapely spy got up, holding her sides, and headed toward the bathroom.

"Ooh, I gotta pee so bad!" She chuckled to herself.

She sat on the commode to relieve herself and literally fell off the seat with more laughter as she looked in the bathtub. Floating in six inches of water was yet another inflated condom with "Portable Navy blow job" lipsticked on it.

Smiling, Fancy picked up the condom, released the drain, turned the shower on, and stepped in.

She grinned at the condom and said to herself, "Natty Tracker, you are a man!"

The stocky middle-aged Korean man said in a loud, commanding voice, *"Chung bi!"*

As one, the class of thirteen black belts and twenty-one brown belts snapped to attention. Divided in four rows, each man and woman, boy and girl, stared straight ahead, feet pointed forward and shoulder-width apart, arms slightly bent, both fists held in front of the abdomen, palms inward.

Garbed in a black belt and white uniform with black piping along the edges, the Korean spoke in broken English, "And just and anyhow . . . I go one month tomorrow back to Seoul and see family-mine. Mr. Tracker in charge. All show Mr. Tracker much respect, same me. Unnerstan?"

The entire class yelled in unison, *"Yes, sir!"*

Natty, standing beside the chief instructor, commanded in Korean, *"Chery up!"*

Everyone brought his feet together, hands against his thighs.

Tracker ordered, *"Chung yeh!"*

The class, including Tracker, bowed as one toward the chief instructor.

The salt-and-pepper-haired man smiled and returned the bow. He winked at Natty and left the room.

Natty faced the class and said, "Okay, everybody scoot back and sit down in front of the mirrors according to rank, except Mr. Deckard. Mr. Deckard, come out for *kata*, please."

"Yes, sir!" came the reply from a young, good-looking first degree black belt.

The curly blond young *karateka* walked out and faced the class, which was seated along a mirrored wall.

Tracker said, *"Chung bi!"*

The man came to the attention position.

Tracker commanded, "Name your first advanced *kata*."

Still staring straight ahead, the young black belt replied, *"Pyong-an chodun*, sir!"

Natty boomed, *"Shi jah!"*

The young black belt exploded to his left in a perfect front stance with a powerful sweeping lower block with his left forearm, followed by a step forward and an explosive reverse punch with his right fist.

He paused for a millisecond and spun backward ending in another perfect front stance with his right fist whipping down in a low block. Then his right fist snapped downward and across his body in a forearm cross-block as his right foot simultaneously slid back in a simulated leg sweep.

"Hold it!" Natty shouted. *"Paroh!"*

The young man stopped and returned to the attention position and then relaxed when Natty said, *"Shuh!"*

Natty walked out of the room and returned carrying a black cloth. He approached the student and tied the cloth around the young man's eyes.

Tracker spoke to the young man, actually addressing the whole class, "That was superb, Mr. Deckard. Your *kata* is always clean, but the one time you need to defend yourself, a gang of intruders may have cut the electricity to your home, and you are in total darkness, fighting for your life. Someone may attack and throw a blinding fluid into your eyes before he tries to kill you. Should you just give up and not defend yourself?"

The entire class reponded, "No, sir!"

Tracker gave young Deckard the commands once more, and he performed the choreographed form. With a blindfold on, the young man's movements were awkward, and he was clumsy and often off balance. He finished and returned to his classmates.

"Put your sparring equipment on," Tracker commanded.

The entire class started donning padded gloves on hands and feet. Soon all were clad in the safety gear, as was Tracker. He motioned for two black belts to come up to the middle of the workout area.

"Listen carefully," Natty said. "This is an advanced class with just brown belts and black belts. Don't ever try this with lower ranking students. Somebody'll get hurt."

Facing the two members of the class, Tracker tied the blindfold around his own eyes.

"Bow to me," he said, and all three bowed. "Fighting position."

All three got into a backstance, which some call the free-fighting position.

"Begin!" Natty shouted.

The black belt on Natty's left, a brawny redhead, immediately tried a thundering sidekick to Tracker's ribcage. Tracker's carefully tuned senses, however, warned him, and he sidestepped the kick and trapped the leg, sweeping the other leg with his right foot. The redhead crashed on his back, both hands and forearms slapping the floor in a breakfall technique. Still holding his leg, Natty executed a stomp to the crotch stopping the blade of his right foot a scant inch from the black belt's unprotected groin.

Hearing a rustle of cloth behind him, he dropped the redhead's leg and executed a back kick, feeling the heel and blade of his foot sink into the second black belt's midsection. The young man, thinking he had Natty cold, dived forward in an attempt at a lunge punch, a do-or-die, full-commitment technique.

Blindfolded, Natty's execution was not as clean and picture perfect as usual, so his kick struck the young *karateka* in mid-lunge. Impaled on the end of Natty's powerful leg, he lost his wind and crashed to the floor, fighting panic, as he tried to breathe again.

Natty removed his blindfold and bowed to the red-head. He then addressed the class.

"If you practice *kata* and basic techniques blind-folded, you will improve your balance, awareness, and coordination," he said. "Additionally, try sparring like this with advanced students. I pray that none of us ever have to use the martial arts to defend ourselves, but if you do, that one time you could be blinded, in a phone booth, have your legs broken, or any number of scenarios. Always train with that in mind: Be prepared for anything."

"Very fuckin' impressive, Kung Fu," a voice slurred as Natty turned.

Standing in the doorway was a well-groomed, well-dressed businessman in his mid-thirties, obviously very intoxicated.

"Karate ain't shit," he hollered as Natty moved quickly through an office door. "I can whip the shit outta any a you candy-ass motherfuckers. C'mon!"

Natty came out of the office a moment later.

The drunk said belligerently, "Where'd you go? Chicken shit son-of-a-bitch. I can kick yer wimpy ass."

"You're probably right," Tracker said, "but you'll have to leave."

"Fuck you!" the drunk replied. "I'm gonna kick yer ass, you limp dick."

"Okay, if that's what you want," Natty said, "I'll meet you out front in the parking lot. Let's go."

"Okay, you pussy. C'mon," the drunk said and staggered out followed by Tracker.

Natty, however, stopped and locked the door as soon as the man was through it. He returned to the class and soon grinned at the sound of pounding on the door.

"Never argue with a drunk," he said. "And remember, avoid fights until your back's against the wall. I called the police when he first came in. They'll be here in a minute or two. All right, line up for on-line sparring!"

The students grinned as a siren approached outside, and then the sound of muffled shouting drifted into the room. Natty turned the class over to another black belt and unlocked the front door to consult with the police.

Suffering a case of "High-G Hickeys," Natty intermittently scratched his neck. He had returned earlier that day from the Red Flag War Games at Nellis Air Force Base in Las Vegas, Nevada. Tracker and his best friend and wing man, Captain Peter "Rabbit" Roberts, had gotten into a "squirrel cage," a simulated dogfight, with a pair of F-16's. There was much fast-paced maneuvering and "Bat turns" as the four expert fighter pilots tried to manipulate their opponents into a position in which they could get radar lock-on.

As usual, Natty and Rabbit had won due to their superior flying skills, reflexes, and teamwork. Because of the overload of G-forces on them, both had developed a skin rash called *petechiasis* but commonly referred to as "Fighter Pilots' Measles" or "High-G Hickeys." They had, however, won the respect and undying admiration of the pilots of the "electric jets" they had battled along with that of the other jet drivers.

Tracker was an over-achiever, and he thought of this as he watched the drunken executive being cuffed and taken away. Natty always drank a blackjack on the rocks, a powerful combination of Johnny Walker Black Label and Jack Daniels, but he never allowed himself to drink more than one per day. He could understand how a person became an alcoholic and felt he might if he didn't always exercise self-control.

Tracker returned to the class.

3.

Fate Is Blind

IT WAS RAINING as Natty locked up the karate school and jumped in his black 1963 split-window Corvette. The classic automobile was powered by a 327 cubic-inch engine and had less than thirty thousand miles on it. Natty was not a materialistic person, but he felt no guilt about spending money on some of life's finer things. He shifted into first gear and eased out of the school parking lot, unaware that events were unfolding elsewhere that were going to drastically alter the course of his life.

Baron was a large German Shepherd. His colors were striking, he had a large black saddle and a black mask, alert ears, and intelligent eyes. He was, however, noisy, having learned at too young an age that he could easily intimidate humans and other animals by simply barking at them and looking ferocious. This trait made Baron very much like many people. He was also adept at breaking his leash by tightening his neck muscles and running at full speed from his doghouse. He knew that the flimsy rope would snap if he did not slow down out of fear of injury. Of course, he didn't actually reason this out, but the result was the same. Baron was loose . . . again. It was raining, but the dog knew that he would have fun if he could find that black and white cat that always came around and walked just out of reach of his snapping, saliva-drenched jaws.

At that same time, Cassie Devon poured the last of her glass of Riunite Lambrusco down her slender throat. It was her fourth glass that evening, and it would not be enough to settle the loneliness she felt. She didn't know that it was a chemically induced feeling caused by her habitual overuse of the sweet-tasting wine. Cassie had no idea that the feelings tormenting her were caused by alcohol abuse; she just knew that enough wine took the loneliness away. She couldn't stand those horrible tormenting feelings that forever plagued her, even when she was at a party or surrounded by fellow employees at work.

Cassie decided to plan ahead and go down to the nearby convenience store and buy two more bottles so she wouldn't run out. She walked down the hallway, stumbled over her bathrobe, and looked in at her sleeping two-year-old daughter, Tiffany. Smiling at the slumbering infant, Cassie tiptoed quietly away, changed, and headed for the garage and her white Toyota Cressida.

Tracker looked down at his dash-mounted radar screen and saw the blip that was Cassie's approaching compact and a much smaller blip that was the drenched German Shepherd, tongue hanging out as he searched for the troublesome cat.

As the two vehicles approached each other, Natty

flashed his brights one time in case the weaving driver was falling asleep at the wheel.

Tracker tried to relax all his muscles, mentally preparing them to go into instantaneous action since the radar blip had shown that the approaching car was swaying erratically on the wet roadway. The roadside movements of the large dog also represented a potential hazard.

Natty's greatest fear materialized when the German Shepherd ran toward the road barking at Cassie's car just as she swerved into Tracker's path. Natty kept his head, as usual, eased the car off the pavement, and neatly fitted it between the guard rail and Cassie's Toyota with just a scant half-inch on each side.

In an instant he was safely past her car and had only to ease back onto the road. But Baron lunged in front of the Corvette. Most drivers might have struck and killed the barking pest, but not Tracker. On impulse, he chanced a slight swerve to the left to avoid striking the dog, but as he feared, the wheels of the sports car caught on the steep berm and the car plunged into a series of rollovers along the edge of the road, its black fiberglass body careening harmlessly over the back of the brown and black guard dog.

By the end of the fifth roll, the classic sports car was reduced to a mass of fiberglass splinters and lay upside down, Tracker pinned beneath it, still confined by his seat belt and struggling to get loose. Then he saw gas trickling from the full gas tank now over his head and slightly to the right.

At the same time, accustomed to thinking clearly and analytically in an emergency situation, Tracker made a mental checklist of his injuries so far as he could determine them. He thought he had a broken leg and some bumps and bruises.

Undaunted or simply too drunk to care, Cassie had escaped unharmed and was traveling toward her neighborhood convenience store, unaware that Tracker had turned on his grill-mounted video camera when he saw the potentially dangerous situation developing. The video camera had captured her license number, which Natty instantly memorized. This helped him later in court since the camera was lying along the road in pieces.

The *coup de grâce* was finally delivered when Baron, angered by the sudden intrusion of humans and their steel monsters, trotted up and started barking and growling viciously into Tracker's bloody, rain-pelted face.

"Get the fuck out of here, you ungrateful, flea-bitten sonofabitch!" Tracker yelled at the snarling Shepherd.

Suddenly realizing the ridiculousness of the situation, Natty broke out in laughter, causing the dog to momentarily stop barking and twist his head with curiosity. This odd sight caused Natty to laugh harder. Even though the laughter hurt, he couldn't help himself as he thought about the fact that he had risked life and limb to save this damned dog, and now that he was pinned under his car, the sonofabitch was trying to bite his fucking head off.

Tracker lay laughing in the pouring rain as cars pulled up and stopped. As usual, people jumped out of their cars but then just stood there and stared at Tracker pinned beneath the wreckage of his classic car. Then suddenly, before Natty had a chance to scream *"No!"* one of the watching idiots pulled out an emer-

4.

Fighting Back

"MAJOR TRACKER, CAN you hear me? Can you hear me, Major?"

"Yes, I can," Natty heard his voice reply out of a thick fog.

Tracker tried to think as he felt his eyes open, but the room in which he was lying was pitch black. Had he been shot down over the Soviet Union? That was the first thought he had. Where was he? The accident . . . the asshole with the emergency flare. His thoughts started to race and he caught himself. He could tell that he was in a hospital bed. But how did he know? The smell of the hospital was a dead giveaway, and what else? Tracker could feel that he was in traction and had a cast on his leg and that his ribs were tightly bound. Someone was in the room with him, but why were the lights off and the curtains closed? It was a woman, but how did he know? The perfume . . . Obsession.

"Am I in a hospital?" he asked calmly.

"Yes, you are, Major Tracker," the husky female voice replied out of the darkness. "You were in an accident. How do you feel?"

"Quite honestly, like I've been in the stomach of a great white shark and he decided to toss his cookies," Tracker mused. "Tell me," he continued, "why do you have the room darkened?"

There was a deafening silence, then out of the darkness . . . no, blackness, came the sexy female voice again, "I'm sorry, Major; the room isn't darkened . . . you are blind."

Natty was not shocked. Somehow, he had known as soon as he'd regained consciousness. Still, the verbalization of the fact hit him in the pit of the stomach. Conditioned to immediately react to any adversity with calmness and humor, he smiled.

"Well, your voice sure sounds sexy," he said with a slight smile. "You don't happen to be wearing any tattoos in Braille that I can check out, do you?"

Her laughter was warm and sincere and Natty tried to imagine a face to put with the voice.

She spoke again, "I'm your doctor, Major Tracker. I'm Captain Leigh . . . Captain Wanda Leigh."

"Yes, I might wanna," Tracker grinned through the veil of pain, "but let's get to know each other better, Doctor."

"Oh boy, it looks like you're going to be a handful, Major," she responded.

Natty chuckled, "I just might be. Play your cards right and you'll find out . . . and please call me Natty or just Tracker."

Poking his big toe, she asked, "Feel this?"

"Yes."

"Good, you can call me Wanda . . . when we're alone." She smiled and looked at his handsome face, sensual fantasies playing in her mind.

Getting serious, Natty asked, "What caused the blindness, and how long will it last?"

Wanda sighed deeply. "Natty, I can tell that you're not the type of man who likes to beat around the bush . . ."

Tracker interrupted with a nasty chuckle, eyes staring unseeing toward the ceiling, "*Au contraire*, Wanda. You've got me wrong there."

The long-limbed doctor laughed vigorously. "Oh God, I really stepped in it, didn't I?" she said. Then she continued in a more serious vein, "Natty, I'm afraid that the blindness is permanent. The concussion of the explosion caused permanent damage to your optic nerve. On the other hand, the police and paramedics said that living through the explosion was miraculous in itself."

"I was just lucky," Tracker replied modestly. "Well, I guess, dear doctor, that it's time for me to drop back ten and punt."

"You certainly take bad news in stride," she said.

Natty smiled as he turned his blank, staring blue eyes toward the shapely doctor. "Well, Wanda, my mother used to tell me to never worry about things that I can't change. And even though these eyes may not work right now, I'll still see again. I just don't believe in 'never.' Now, Wanda, tell me what you look like. Better yet, why don't you come over here and let me see you with my hands?"

Wanda sat down on the edge of Tracker's bed, and he reached up slowly and softly ran his fingertips over her face.

"Soft lips," Tracker said as Wanda's breasts heaved. "Soft skin, too . . . cute nose, high cheekbones, an uplift to your chin. Your self-esteem is good."

"You sure are learning to live with your handicap very quickly," Wanda said.

Tracker smiled. "Right now, I wouldn't refer to it as a handicap." He moved his hands higher and caressed her hair. "Your hair is thick and naturally curly and very long. It's black, you have an olive complexion, and your eyes are very dark brown . . . almost black . . . right?"

"I'm impressed, Tracker," she cooed. "How did you figure all that out?"

Natty smiled again. "Lucky guess," he answered. Her breathing quickened as his hand slowly slid down her neck. "Oh, slim neck. And feminine but athletic shoulders. You're right-handed and you play a lot of tennis or racquetball, correct?"

"How can you tell?"

"Muscular development in your shoulders and a little guesswork," he replied. "May I, Doctor?"

Trying to control her breathing, Wanda paused. "Natty, I want you to know that I normally don't allow myself to get familiar with patients."

Natty just grinned and said softly, "Doctor, I'm just looking at you like all your other patients do. I'm just using my fingers instead of my eyes. May I, Doctor?"

She paused again . . . and finally spoke with a frog in her throat, "Well, Natty, I've acted this unprofessionally already, and orders have been issued to the nurses that you're not to be disturbed. You might as well finish looking at me."

She tensed as his hand moved very slowly as he smiled and said, "Firm breasts . . . good abdomen . . . nice hips."

"Oh, Natty," she sighed, "if you only knew how you're making me feel inside."

Natty grinned broadly. "Come closer, Doctor, let's have a look."

As his hand moved softly into the moistness of her most private secrets, she purred heavily. He pulled her close and their lips met . . . and soon their tongues swirled like electric jets in a dogfight. She lay down and pushed herself against his hardness.

Grinning confidentally, Tracker whispered, "Well, Doctor Leigh, if I'm to get better, we'd better start my therapy sessions right now."

"I agree, Natty," she moaned. "Oh, I agree!"

Natty murmured, "As a matter of fact, you're acting like you could use an injection from 'Doctor Feelgood' yourself."

Tracker had to remain in the hospital for two weeks, and during that time, he and Wanda has as many "therapy sessions" as possible. It was probably the main reason for his relatively quick recovery.

For the next several months, Tracker learned how to function without sight, and even went back to classes in Tae Kwon Do. The only part of his new lifestyle that really bothered him was the fact that he was given a medical retirement from the Air Force. It had been his life, and he absolutely loved flying jets.

His money from the Tracker System and other inventions he'd sold to the government had been kept in a blind trust for him, since he didn't want to be accused of having a conflict of interests. The money, in the millions, bought Tracker every gadget designed for the blind currently on the market. If Tracker had chosen to, he could have lived in luxury the rest of his days, but Natty knew that money could not buy true satisfaction or adrenaline highs. He needed both to function properly in life.

He started working on his own, and the first invention he developed was based on the simple sonar of the bat. Tracker fashioned a miniature earplug that was hidden in his left ear and had a wire running behind the ear to the frame of a pair of sunglasses. Inside was a microchip that took sonar readings fed to it through a miniaturized transmitter receiver that sent sound waves out from the front of the glasses and timed how quickly they returned. The sonic intervals were translated into beeps in Tracker's ear. The closer an object, the faster the beeps. The larger the object, the deeper the pitch of the beep. After learning to use this simple but ingenious device, Tracker was soon able to walk through a crowded room without bumping into anyone. Natty called this latest development SOD, for Sonar Orientation Device.

He started using the SOD in his Tae Kwon Do classes and was able to spar effectively against other students. Next, he tried using it out in the country, driving a dirt bike, but he found that the front fender and handlebars created too much interference with the sonic pulses. Natty went back to the drawing board to redesign the SOD so it would enable its user to drive any kind of vehicle.

After two months, he finally discovered that the microchip in the sonar device could be programmed to ignore certain parameters of sonic feedback created by the vehicle in which the wearer was traveling. Thinking positively and toward the future, Natty devised a method to couple his sonar device to the radar systems of a jet aircraft.

His friend Rabbit, a constant visitor, was concerned

when he learned of this latest development. When he asked Tracker why he dared dream so big, Natty just shrugged and chuckled.

Turning to face Rabbit by locating him with the sonar beeps, Tracker grinned and said, "Rabbit, some people can see so well that they become blind."

5.

Blind Injustice

NATTY STILL FOUND walking in urban areas difficult due to the traffic, curbs, and pedestrians, so he carried a white cane with a red tip. He was going to meet Wanda for dinner at a restaurant in downtown Anchorage. The air was nippy but not uncomfortably cold.

Unfortunately, Tracker didn't know his proposed route to the restaurant crossed the turf of some would-be hard cases who hassled anyone they felt they could intimidate. A blind man with a white cane coming down the street was too much for them to resist.

Natty smelled trouble once he was in their midst. As they closed in around him, he halted and smiled.

"Yo—mothahfuckah," the leader said, "we want yo' fuckin' wallet, man."

Tracker grinned broadly and said, "Move apart and get out of my way."

"What you mean, 'move apart,' Stevie Wonder?" the leader asked. "What makes you think there's more than just me?"

Tracker grinned even more broadly. "Because I know that punks like you don't have the balls to stand up one on one, man to man. That's why you and your pussy friends have to form gangs. You know . . . safety in numbers.''

"Man, I'm gonna bust yo' mothahfuckin' head,'' the leader raged as the gang members prodded him on. "Ain't no fuckah ever talks to me like that, blind or not. I don't give a fuckin' shit, I'm gonna grease yo' fuckin' ass, blind man.''

Still grinning, Natty raised his hand, temporarily halting the now-advancing thugs, who stood awed by his calmness.

He said, "Look, contrary to popular opinion, I'm not required to tell you this, but I'm a black belt in karate, and I only fight to defend myself. You guys seem bound and determined to attack me, so if you do, let's know where we're comin' from. I view it as a life-or-death situation, so if I kill any of you, tough shit. Now that's my ground rule. We can all just walk away if you want.''

The gang, all eight of them, stood looking at each other, rebuilding their courage. This and his short speech gave Natty time to pinpoint each one with his sonar and quickly formulate a plan of attack. He knew his speech would make them less effective fighters, since it would frighten them to some degree and make them a little hesitant in the face of his confidence, even though he was blind.

The leader pulled out a switchblade, opened it, and snarled "You a dead mothahfuck . . . Ahh!''

Natty's crescent kick swept up from the street in a vicious arc and the edge of his shoe badly bruised the leader's wrist and sent the knife sailing into the street. As soon as his foot touched the sidewalk, Natty skipped forward and sent it back up in an opposite arc that crashed into the leader's temple, sending him sprawling unconscious into two other gang members.

Natty sensed one lunging at him from behind and struck the man with a vicious back kick; at the same time, he heard one directly in front of him and jabbed straight forward with the handle of his cane, imbedding it in the man's throat just below the Adam's apple. The thug went down with a strangled gurgling sound emanating from him. The one who was back-kicked had three broken ribs and a punctured lung.

Natty then pinpointed one rushing at him from his left front and another straight to his rear. Out of intuition more than anything else, he did a quick rising block and felt a club break over his forearm. He executed a fast snap kick to his left front and felt it catch somebody under the chin. Without setting his foot down, he immediately sent it backward full force in another back kick and heard the assailant scream as the foot crushed his kneecap. When he front kicked the other one, he felt and heard the chin break and knew that at least several teeth had been knocked out.

Sensing another attacker to his immediate front, but not knowing that the punk, scared to death, was trying to back away, Tracker decided to really intimidate the others. With a loud yell, he jumped up, spun high into the air, and lunged his right foot out in a spinning back kick that caught the man on the shoulder and badly bruised it. Landing, Natty lashed out with a left-handed backfist to the man's nose and felt the cartilage give way. This was followed a split-second later by a right-handed reverse punch to the heart that broke a rib, and then a back-foot round kick that almost tore the assailant's head off and sent him to the ground unconscious.

Tracker stood up straight, grinning again, and said

to the remaining punks, "Okay, I'm warmed up. Let's get serious now; no more fucking around."

They took off at a dead run down the street, leaving their fallen comrades for the cops, vultures, or whatever. They were too frightened to care. Tracker heard the injured ones on the ground around him moaning, and two were crying.

The leader said from the ground, "Shit, man, you ain't fuckin' blind. What are you, Batman or somethin'?"

Tracker laughed, "No, pal, but you sure as hell aren't the Joker, either."

By this time, Tracker was able to calm down and focus on his other surroundings. He could tell that some passing cars had stopped and some onlookers had come out of nearby buildings.

In a loud voice, he commanded, "Call the police and an ambulance!"

Somebody already had, because he had no sooner said it than he heard distant sirens. The fight itself had lasted less than thirty seconds, but in a situation like that, time seems to stand still. Tracker was really up now . . . a pure adrenaline high.

Inside, his nerves were also short-circuiting, but he had long ago learned how to control that. He got sensations of nausea, diarrhea, cramps, shakiness, and light-headedness. All of this was caused by his nervous system. He had just been in battle. He had faced injury or death against multiple opponents and had vanquished them. Tracker knew what it was like after a battle, so he pressed himself beyond those feelings, accepted them, and didn't worry about it.

To the bystanders watching him now, he was ten feet tall and looked to be totally undaunted by the situation.

This blind man had defeated, absolutely humiliated, the gang of toughs that had for so long terrorized their neighborhood.

One old sourdough had walked out of a nearby bar with another and had seen most of the confrontation. He pointed at Tracker and said to his partner, "Now Buck, yonder there stands a man."

6.

Moving and Digging In

AFTER ANOTHER ALASKAN winter, Tracker said good-bye to his friends in Anchorage and moved south.

Colorado Springs, Colorado, at the foot of majestic Pike's Peak, was fast becoming a major center of technology. It was centrally located and noted for relatively mild winters. It was the home of the Air Force Academy, Peterson Air Force Base, Fort Carson Army Base, and was the headquarters of NORAD, the North American Air Defense Command. Located deep within the bowels of hollowed-out Cheyenne Mountain, NORAD headquarters rests on massive shock absorbers for stability during an earthquake or nuclear attack. Protected by the solid rock of the mountain and thick steel doors that can withstand a direct blast from a low-yield nuclear bomb, and filled with the most modern computer technology, NORAD is the brain center of America's defense systems. It would also be the future site of many of Tracker's meetings with high government officials in connection with the business venture he was planning.

Natty bought a palatial house at the base of Cheyenne mountain, near the world-famous Broadmoor Hotel, and started working on inventions in earnest. At night, he usually took Air Force generals and other government officials out to dinner to make contacts and get his name known.

Tracker continued to improve his SOD glasses and his ability to function and orient himself with their sonar readings.

He also started work on his most important invention . . . the OPTIC System. Working with several opthamologists and scientists he flew in, Natty devised a revolutionary system. OPTIC stood for Optical Tracking Initiation Contrivance, and the basic mechanics weren't tremendously difficult to develop. Natty's problem, however, was the very delicate laser surgery needed to find out if the device worked effectively. Not only was this surgery revolutionary, costly, dangerous, and very experimental, it was illegal as well. No one had even considered this type of eye surgery, let alone performed it on laboratory animals.

Natty had only one choice; he called his contacts in Washington and set up a meeting. With a noted opthamologist, two research doctors, and a well-known scientist in tow, he booked a flight to Washington. After a short commuter hop to Stapleton International Airport near Denver, the five were soon jetting through the crisp night sky.

Smiling, Natty turned to the doctor seated next to him in the first class cabin and said, "How appropriate."

The opthamologist looked puzzled and said, "I don't understand, Natty."

"The flight we're on," replied Tracker, "is the 'red eye,' Doctor."

They laughed.

* * *

The following day found the five in a long meeting with officials from the National Security Council, CIA, FBI, and the Pentagon. All felt that Tracker's business plans for the near future would be helpful to them, but they also were certain the OPTIC System was incredible, revolutionary, and so far-fetched that it had little chance of success. Nevertheless, Tracker convinced them that it was his own head on the operating table and that he was a big boy, so they consented secretly to the surgery, with the provisos that there be no lawsuits if the operation failed and no publicity if it were successful. The latter was to give the government time to study and experiment before exposing the public to such a potentially dangerous procedure.

Less than a week later, Tracker lay on an operating table surrounded by a team of eye surgeons, nurses, and medical technicians. A microchip was implanted behind each eye and fiberoptic filaments attached to the optic nerves. Two more leads from each microchip were brought out of the rim of each eye socket, under the facial tissue, and both emerged through the eyebrows. These were to be used to plug into the frames of Natty's SOD glasses that had been radically modified to interface with the rest of the OPTIC System.

It took some weeks of bedrest and recovery before the glasses could be tested. The doctors also wanted to make sure Tracker's body would accept the foreign material implanted in it. Those weeks of healing were boring, painful, and very anxious for Tracker, but they passed, and he healed well.

The time finally came for Tracker to try out the rest of the system. With his fellow experimenters looking on, Natty put the glasses on, and the leads were attached. In the frames was a miniaturized transceiver system that transmitted to and received information from Tracker's mainframe IBM computer at his home. It then sent electrical impulses to the microchips behind Tracker's eyes that processed them and transmitted a biocompatible signal to the filaments implanted in the optic nerves. The lenses of the sunglasses themselves were similar to video camera lenses. By stimulating the optic nerves behind the retina of each eye in the pattern seen by the lenses, Tracker was able to see an outline of everything he looked at. Like a camera, Tracker had no depth perception, but that could be compensated for with the sonar SOD System. The principle worked very much like video in that the electrical impulses stimulated the optic nerves in the outline of whatever Natty's glasses were focused on. He could not actually see objects or people, but saw the outline in a dot-matrix pattern. He also could only see in a sort of black and white, but when things were very close, the nerves received more impulses, causing the object to appear reddish.

Over the next six months, Natty not only practiced "seeing" with the SOD and OPTIC Systems, he also improved upon the OPTIC System, adding a night-vision capability by enabling the system to gather and amplify available starlight and moonlight to create a daylight-quality field of vision.

At the same time, Tracker began to fly again, but not in his beloved F-15C Eagle. He bought a twin-engine Beechcraft and a powerful single-engine Cessna. Natty fitted both with state-of-the-art radar and sonar to which he adapted the SOD/OPTIC Systems by reconfiguring them to electronically interface with his multi-million-dollar glasses.

Tracker would not be satisfied until he was flying a monster machine with a pair of Pratt and Whitney's throwing him through his own little corridor of space at speeds that would make most grown men weep and cry for their mothers. Learning to fly again was easier for Tracker than moving around on two legs. His "touch-and-go's" were flawless, and Natty gave a whole new meaning to IFR flight, but he didn't allow himself to become complacent.

His mind was locked on one ultimate goal, and that was to be a jet driver once again. He had learned years before the relatively simple way to achieve success in any endeavor. That was to set an objective, work harder than anybody else toward it, and never give up no matter what you encounter. Tracker had always had a problem understanding how so many people could not grasp this simple formula for success in life. He had finally concluded that although many did understand what it took, most of them were simply unwilling to exert the effort required.

By this time, Tracker had also gotten into the habit of scratching the telltale scar on his left ring finger he'd gotten in the car wreck. Coincidentally, the scar was shaped precisely like a capital T.

7.

Starting Business

THE ROAD HAD been rough and rocky, long and frustrating at times, but Tracker was finally ready to start business.

He went to Washington for a series of meetings and a very enjoyable several days of cavorting under the covers, on the coffee table, under the kitchen table, and so on with the good Doctor Fancy Bird. It was established that Tracker's main contact, the man from whom he received his orders, would be Wally Rampart, an Undersecretary of State, and a retired Army major general with a reputation as an ass-kicker. His principal function as Tracker's contact was to be the "fall guy," if the need arose, for the President should covert operations be exposed that embarassed the White House.

Wally Rampart was bald, built like a twenty-five-year-old defensive tackle for the Bears, and was a consummate worrier. He was loyal to a fault, both up and down the line, and knew how to kiss some ass when he had to. He was the sort of man who was very selective about the asses he chose to kiss. Wally had many friends in high places and was respected by all who knew him, including his enemies. His nickname, behind his back, was "the Walrus" because of his large brown moustache. Wally would prove to be one of the most valuable "corner men" that Natty could have wished for in Washington.

One of the stories about Undersecretary Rampart around Capitol Hill was the tale of one of his exploits as a battalion commander with the 82nd Airborne at Fort Bragg, North Carolina. On a jump with his troops over Normandy Drop Zone, he found himself on a C-130 Hercules with one of his young riflemen, a PFC from Augusta, Georgia, named Gary Collins, banging, unconscious, against the tail section of the large aircraft. Halfway down his "stick" while jumping out the starboard door of the C-130, Private Collins, on his "cherry" jump, his first drop after airborne training and his sixth jump ever, had exited the door of the aircraft with a vigorous leap into the prop wash, but he had a very weak body position, his elbows out and his eyes closed tightly. The turbulent thrust from the powerful prop blast had wrapped him and his static line around the tangled collection of spent static lines spinning and thrashing against the camouflaged skin of the aircraft.

SFC King Morgan from Harlem, New York, stood in the doorway of the plane looking out at the young trooper. Sergeant Morgan watched, rigger knife in hand, for some sign of consciousness from Private Collins. If Collins were conscious, he was supposed to put his hand on top of his helmet and Morgan would cut the line to let Collins fall away safely so he could open the reserve parachute on his abdomen. Unfortunately, Private Collins simply beat against the craft like a limp ragdoll, and Sergeant Morgan didn't know what to do.

That's when then-Lieutenant Colonel Wally Rampart took over. Grabbing the rigger's knife from a protesting Sergeant Morgan, Wally quickly grabbed his own fifteen-foot static line and tied it in a slip knot in his parachute harness. Then, holding the knife between his teeth, he crawled hand over hand down his static line, and banging viciously against the plane himself, he cut the bird's nest of twisted lines away from the limp soldier. He wrapped his arms and legs tightly around the unconscious young paratrooper and reached up to yank the slip knot out of his static line. His parachute opened smoothly, and he held his young charge all the way down to the sandy drop zone.

The one thing that was different about this particular story on Capitol Hill was that it was true. Wally had received the Soldier's Medal for his actions, which looked good with his three Purple Hearts, two Silver Stars, four Bronze Stars, and the other awards collected over his illustrious career. As a captain and a company commander with the 173rd Airborne in South Vietnam, Wally had been the type of commander that Hollywood screenwriters liked to pattern their heros after.

Phil Herbert had worked for the government for seventeen years and knew how to keep his mouth shut. That was one reason he had a Top Secret security clearance. He had one more telephone extension to install in the mammoth home, and he looked at his surroundings and admired the rustic, masculine look of the furnishings. He knew that the ''safe'' phones he was installing with the automatic encoding devices would connect the blind guy he had seen in Washington. He couldn't figure out why this blind guy was such a big-shot, but he liked him. The guy seemed like a man's man, really in control and down to earth; besides his pad looked like the kind he himself dreamed about.

Phil did his job and didn't try to guess too much. His professional philosophy was very simple: Don't worry about knowing too much and then you won't have to worry about leaking something accidentally.

One thing Phil didn't know was that he had been followed to Colorado Springs from Washington. He didn't know that the businessman across the aisle on his flight had been picked up by another one in a non-descript blue Plymouth that had followed him and the FBI field agent who had dropped him off at Tracker's home and was to pick him up in precisely one hour's time. He didn't know that the Soviet KGB knew that this "unimportant" government worker installed tele-phones in the homes of VIPs who dealt with the gov-ernment on classified projects.

The two KGB agents were parked a block and a half from Tracker's house and were soon joined by a phony Roto-Rooter truck. Watching the house carefully, they entered the truck, which was an electronic spy head-quarters on wheels. A camouflaged dish-shaped micro-phone was aimed at Tracker's windows. The spies soon learned that Natty's home was equipped with triple panes. Ordinarily the super-sensitive directional an-tenna would have been able to pick up conversations within the house from sound waves vibrating against the windows. Unfortunately, the electronic spies were only able to hear gentle Muzak piped in between the outer and middle panes of glass.

An hour after setting up, the four Soviets in the

truck's interior were startled to hear a knock on the back door of the truck. While two of the Soviet agents drew American-made .357 Magnum Colt Pythons, the agent in charge, dressed in a Roto-Rooter uniform, opened the back door slightly. He was handed two large pizzas in cardboard boxes by a Domino's Pizza delivery man.

The smiling young man said, "Sir, I was told to give you a message from a Mister Tracker. He said to tell you to keep up the good work, and he said that he hopes you like anchovies on your pizzas and he's sorry he couldn't send vodka, but he wanted you to have these two large bottles of Coke anyway."

The agent in charge, Yuri, started laughing, said, "Thank you," and closed the door.

He handed the pizzas to his compatriots after extracting the first slice for himself, and speaking in his native tongue, said, "Comrades, I believe we are going to enjoy maintaining surveillance on this Nathaniel Tracker a lot more than previous targets. I am certain that it will not be as boring."

Tracker's new business was the end result of the natural evolution of his life. Summoned whenever needed and equipped with his vast experience, keen mind, and most importantly, his varied inventions, Natty was hired by the US Government as the ultimate Tracker . . . the supreme private investigator. If the Navy should lose a nuclear warhead, Natty would be one of the first summoned to find it. If the CIA lost classified documents, he was hired to track them down.

Most of his work would be classified, jobs that might be embarassing to the government if a government employee were involved, so Natty always worked as an independent contractor paid from a secret State Department account controlled by Wally Rampart. If Natty received orders from the President, he wouldn't really know it since everything was channeled through General Rampart.

His first assignment was simple as far as Natty was concerned. The government wanted to locate the hide-out of a retired Central American general who had been smuggling drugs into the United States. First, Natty checked with the DEA and found out who the primary US purchasers were for the general's drugs. He then hired a retired US Army Special Forces officer who had turned character actor and part-time military technical advisor for motion pictures to set up a meeting with the general's top buyer, an Irishman named Paddy O'Neil who had moved to the United States with his parents at the age of five. By the age of ten, he had knifed his first man in a dark alley in New York's Hell's Kitchen area. The man, trying to earn some extra money while attending college, was working as a number's runner and had made the mistake of not taking seriously a ten-year-old boy who was going on thirty.

Referred with a stamp of approval by a DEA agent who was under deep cover, the retired officer/actor had a meeting with Paddy in which he carefully made vague references to the difficulties of getting foreign foodstuffs and the like through customs. He showed Paddy a series of suitcases, briefcases, and overnight bags that could not be opened without the proper keys. Each piece had a lead-lined secret compartment built in, and the liners were soaked with a special recipe of herbs and spices to distract customs dogs used to sniff out illegal "foodstuffs." The luggage was very, very expensive, but damned well worth it. This was followed by the viewing of a phony videotape of a drug-sniffing dog supposedly fooled by the luggage.

Stupidly, Paddy, who wouldn't have been a criminal if he'd been intelligent, bought every piece of luggage that the actor had to offer. The cost turned out to be the tidy sum of $42,000 which Tracker allowed the actor to keep as a bonus.

What poor Paddy didn't know was that implanted within the handle of each piece of luggage was a microchip that gave off an inaudible high-frequency beep. When DEA undercover agents reported that a big drug buy was going down between Paddy and the general, Mohawk airplanes with ultrasensitive direction-finding radio equipment flew constantly in the area, always in pairs. Each implanted microchip had a separate frequency, and the planes maintained a computerized azimuth on each chip. When the drug buy went down, Paddy made the payment with three of the suitcases, and it was a simple matter to keep track of their whereabouts and home in on their ultimate destination: the hideout of the general.

Not long after, Tracker received the first feather for his new cap, and rumor had it that the general had been killed by a letter bomb, probably by a jealous competitor from Columbia. Strangely enough, the general's followers believed all they read, even what US intelligence leaked to the press to deceive them. The Columbian competitor, another elusive drug lord, was found in his bathtub, his throat slit and his tongue sticking through the gaping slash.

When, over a cup of coffee at a little restaurant named Baron's near Cheyenne Mountain, Natty was told of these final events by Wally Rampart, he grinned slyly, took a long sip of steaming coffee, and said, "General, the Chinese say, 'When the bird has been killed, the bow is put away; after the rabbit has been killed, the hunting dog goes into the cooking pot.' I believe that applies here."

8.

The Honey Badger

THE TALL ELEPHANT grass waved across the veldt like green breakers in a silky emerald sea. The large bull elephant smelled a waterhole, not much more than a mud puddle, a full three miles away across the plain. The wrinkled trunk of the old elephant rose and blasted a signal to the other members of his herd as he took off at a trot. Then the bull suddenly brayed in agony and stood paralyzed by pain.

Moments before, a small bundle of fur had launched itself from between the elephant's hind legs and was now attached to the big bull's scrotum. White fur on the top and dark fur on the bottom half, the animal, nearly as large as a medium-sized dog, with short stubby legs, growled viciously as it tore angrily at the pachyderm's testicles. Refusing to let go of the huge bull's groin, the little killer finally tore the crotch loose and dropped to the ground as the elephant trumpeted in pain, fury, and fear.

The small mammal scrambled off into the brush to escape the monster's wrath.

Many outdoorsmen consider the wolverine the meanest, most vicious animal on earth. Others consider the great white shark deserving of that title and still others the grizzly bear or the Cape buffalo. Those biologists, naturalists, and big game guides who really know the animals of Africa, though, feel that the title singularly belongs to the honey badger. This mean little killer will attack elephants, rhinos, and Cape buffalo by hiding in the grass, jumping up, and biting out the large animal's groin just out of meanness. They then hide in the bush and watch their victims bleed to death, writhing in pain.

The Africaaner term for the honey badger is "The Ratel" which was the nickname given Pedro Carlos Jesus Rodriguez Jimenez de Habana. The nickname was applied to the Cuban guerrilla by the world's intelligence community after many heinous crimes against humanity. Pedro claimed to be the bastard son of the late Ché Guevara, probably the best-known guerrilla leader of the twentieth century, who helped lead the Cuban revolution that put Fidel Castro in power. In actuality, however, The Ratel was the bastard son of an Havana-born prostitute and who-knows-which-one of thousands of itinerate cane laborers.

Unlike Ché Guevara, who wore a variety of disguises and traveled freely from Communist revolution to Communist revolution in both South America and Africa, The Ratel was a hard person to camouflage. He stood six feet ten inches tall and weighed 413 pounds, most of it muscle, and sported an horrendous scar that ran from his left ear to the corner of his mouth. There it created a pucker that made him look like he was always trying to suppress a smile. This hideous scar had been caused by the premature explosion of a letter bomb he had been preparing to send to the Pope, just to see how many hands the bomb would go through

before it detonated. He was practicing one of his grue-
some terrorist techniques just for fun.

After the letter bomb explosion, The Ratel special-
ized in kidnapping and assassination, using his hands,
knives, and guns, but he shied away from all explosive
devices. Like his hero, Ché, he hired out to any country
or group that was anti-USA, and as long as he could
practice terrorism and get paid, he was happy. He pretended to believe in the cause of whatever entity that
hired him, but his only real cause was perpetuating the
legend of "The Ratel."

Pedro had been sent to Nicaragua to "do some work"
for that government. Their intelligence reports had located a Contra rebel cadre, and the government wanted
them eliminated. Instead of killing the three men, Pedro decided to torture them first and let them die slowly.
The first was pinpointed in a camouflaged hut in the
jungle just two kilometers from his village. He was so
close because his young wife was due to deliver her
second child, and the first had been a breech birth. The
Ratel came to the village, took the rebel leader's wife
hostage, and when she went into labor, he tied her legs
together firmly at the ankles and let her screams bring
the leader to him. Later, the wife's throat was slit and
the man was beheaded with a pocketknife. The Ratel
found the other two rebel leaders and executed them in
a similar manner.

Although Pedro worshipped Ché Guevara, he failed
to appreciate that Ché met his death in South America
at the hands of some ill-equipped soldiers guided by
US Army Green Beret advisors who had hounded Ché
all over the world. At the time of his death, the Communist guerrilla was covered with sores and suffering
from malnutrition and pneumonia. Ché Guevara was

simply a thug, a punk killer who operated ruthlessly and met a lonely, miserable death in a deserted jungle far from his home. The Ratel was the same sort of degenerate but he had more advanced weapons and many more countries willing to hire him to disrupt the free world.

At that time, The Ratel was in the employ of another punk and terrorist named Colonel Muammar al-Qaddafi, the leader of Libya, and more commonly referred to by most American intelligence types as "Wacky Qaddafi."

In the summer of 1989, the Hasballah, in retaliation for the Israeli kidnapping of their leader, announced to the world press that they had executed American hostage Marine Lieutenant Colonel John Higgins and subsequently released a videotape showing his body hanging from a noose. One of the military measures US leaders ordered was buzzing the borders of several terrorist states by US Naval and Air Force jets. This was to get states such as Libya and Iraq to activate hidden radar sites. In this way, the US got a reading on those sites for possible destruction in case of a US air strike.

One thing that did not make the papers was that one air force pilot, by a fluke, was shot down over Libya and taken prisoner. The pilot had taken extreme risks that day buzzing Libyan positions. The Libyans fired heat-seeking ground-to-air missiles at him, but he'd smoothly evaded them with high-G acrobatics and by releasing parachute flares to attract the missiles. However, he'd run out of flares and two Soviet-made SAM missiles had been fired at him simultaneously. He had managed to dodge one but not the other. The American ace had ejected from his flaming F-15C Eagle without a scratch to float softly down to the Libyan desert, landing atop a Libyan army barracks with hundreds of AK-47 assault rifles pointed at him.

Raising his hands, the pilot had chuckled and simply said, "Where the fuck is Superman when you need him? Shooting steel bolts into Lois Lane's pussy."

The pilot, who had volunteered for the dangerous mission, was a jet jockey from Elmendorf Air Force Base near Anchorage, Alaska. His name was Captain Peter "Rabbit" Roberts . . . and he was now in the sinister hands of The Ratel.

9.

Tracking the Rabbit

THE US AIR Force C-141 Starlifter whistled to a stop on the tarmack of the Tripoli International Airport in Libya. The ground crew drove out to greet the plane with a contingent of Libyan soldiers.

Not far away, out in the gulf, US Naval F-14 Tomcats sat waiting on the deck of an aircraft carrier in case they had to fly in and bail out the big jet.

The ground crew drove a cargo cart up to the massive loading door on the rear of the jet. With a creak and a groan from its hydraulics, the ramp went down slowly and two crewmen jumped off to supervise the unloading. Three wooden caskets, nailed tight, were carefully unloaded onto the cargo cart while the American and Libyan crews eyed each other with suspicion. Wailing could be heard from a cluster of family members beyond the eight-foot cyclone and barbed wire security fence. The mourners beat themselves on the head and thrashed themselves with sticks as they cried. The cart slowly made its way toward the terminal as the ramp closed on the large jet.

The giant turbines on the monster jet whistled ner-

vously like a big dumb kind tiptoeing through a grave-
yard as the C-141 crept slowly toward the runway and
the relative safety of the blue desert sky. Near the peak
of hysteria, at the edge of a shadowy cemetery, the
cargo jet screamed with panic and one could almost
hear it saying to itself, "Feet, don't fail me now!" as
it ran blindly down the runway, jumped off the end,
and "got the hell out of Dodge."

Inside the airport the three caskets were claimed by
crying, wailing family members. Each casket was taken
off in a different direction. The three bodies within were
Libyan fishermen who had sunk far out in the Gulf of
Sidra. Fishing out of the old port city of Homs, their
boat had apparently capsized during a freak storm, but
no one knew for certain. Perhaps they simply bumped
into Wacky Qaddafi's "Invisible Line of Death." The
bodies had been picked up by an American naval ship
and arrangements had been made to return them for
burial. This had been done privately through diplomatic
channels, while publicly, the good colonel had tried to
claim that the US sank the tiny fishing boat. Privately,
an American-educated Libyan diplomat had thanked the
Americans for their assistance, while secretly referring
to his leader as "the Archie Bunker of the Islamic
world."

Two of the caskets were loaded into the back of an
old rusty one-ton pickup truck that started out immediately for Homs, while the third was placed inside a
1956 Ford station wagon that had been converted into
a hearse. The curtains on the windows were closed, and
two of the three men who had picked up the casket slid
into the back next to the coffin while the third drove
toward the busy downtown section of Tripoli. All three
had been educated at American universities, held po-

sitions in the Libyan government, and wanted nothing more than to normalize relations with the United States. They considered Qaddafi a madman who was rushing their country rapidly backward to the sixteenth century and wanted him gone. They had all done minor intelligence work for the CIA, but did it with the thought that they were helping their country, which they loved dearly, not causing it harm.

They were now garbed in the robes of the working class. One tapped on the lid of the wooden casket, and another series of taps echoed from within. One of them took a crowbar and started prying the lid open. With a creak, the last nail finally let go, a pair of dark-skinned hands opened it all the way, and up sat Natty Tracker, an oxygen mask over his smiling mouth. He removed the mask and shook hands all around while stretching out his cramped limbs.

The leader/spokesman for the three said, "Welcome to our country. We were told to help you, but we do not know why you are here. I am Mohammad Ubari."

Tracker said, "Mohammad, pleased to meet you. Name's Natty Tracker. I'm here to locate and rescue an American jet pilot who was shot down, and we've heard he's being held and questioned by The Ratel."

"I've heard of such a thing," Mohammad replied, "but they flew away without wings. We do not know where to find them."

Tracker smiled, "I know the desert holds a thousand secrets, Mohammad, but surely men of your obvious intelligence and standing can find out where he's being held."

Mohammad laughed and said, "Tracker, we will do our best, but not because you are trying to stroke our egos. We want the United States to know that not everybody who lives here is an uncivilized asshole. Do we understand each other?''

Embarrassed, Natty laughed heartily, "Mohammad, I not only understand you, more importantly, I respect you.''

They took Tracker to a tiny room in downtown Tripoli, where he hid out for three days while they came and went at varying intervals. He was never told the names of the other two, nor did they converse with him, although it was obvious they understood English. Natty figured they were smart enough to use Mohammad as their spokesman and felt no need to give more information about themselves that could be revealed under interrogation.

On the third evening, Mohammad entered the room wearing a conservative business suit and a toothy smile.

His black eyes flashed as he addressed Tracker. "We have learned, my friend, where the American pilot is being held: the Fortress of the Angry Sands. It is just outside the city.''

"Good going, Mohammad," Natty responded enthusiastically. "What is this fortress? Can you take me there?''

"Of course, I can take you. We can leave at once,'' Mohammad replied. "It is an old military fortress from times past. The walls are very high, not only for defense, but also because it is a very windy area. The desert around there wears a new face every day . . . sometimes every hour.''

"What have you heard about my fr—the American?'' Natty asked as they each wrapped themselves in a sackcloth garment called a *baraccan* and walked out into the night air.

The pair jumped into an old Citroën as Mohammad answered, "He has been tortured but is alive. I know they do not plan to let him live too much longer, especially since they tortured him. His name is Peter Roberts and he is a captain in your air force."

As soon as they arrived, Natty's heart sank. Located on the outskirts of Tripoli, the old stone fort had walls that looked to be seventy-five feet high, and there were armed guards evenly spaced at fifty-foot intervals all the way around the fort. There was no way it could be approached without detection from any direction.

Getting into the fort looked to be impossible and Mohammad thought of this as he glanced at the man next to him with the strange-looking glasses and hearing aid in his left ear. Mohammad had been trying to figure out this unusual American, but he sensed that Tracker did not view getting into the fort as an impossible feat, or even anything worse than inconvenient. He felt a quiet strength emanating from this man. He had never seen Tracker with the fancy sunglasses off, but whenever Tracker talked to him, Mohammad felt the glasses were special goggles enabling Tracker to look straight into his soul. He shivered and looked back at the shadowy structure.

"All the guards are carrying automatic weapons with plenty of extra clips," Natty observed.

"You can see that?" Mohammad exclaimed.

Natty smiled, "Eat lots of carrots."

"Huh?"

"Nothing," Tracker replied. "C'mon, let's go. Nothing we can do here. Can we head to the sea?"

"Of course," Mohammad said and turned north.

The beat up little Citroën made it to the edge of the crystal clear Mediterranean, and at Natty's request turned eastward and rolled along near the blue sea. At a secluded stretch, Natty asked to be dropped off.

"Here?" Mohammad said incredulously. "Should I wait for you? It is like a camel stopping in the middle of the desert to drink sand."

Tracker laughed as the little car braked to a halt. "Naw," he replied, "just come by tomorrow morning and pick me up if I'm still here. I like to walk by the water and think."

Tracker grabbed his small duffle and jumped out as Mohammad asked, "And if you are not here, Tracker?"

Natty smiled warmly and stuck out his hand and shook with the Libyan agent. He stepped back from the car and gave a wave as a signal for Mohammad to leave.

Reaching into his duffle, Tracker pulled out a can of shaving cream and a disposable razor. He popped the nozzle off the can with his thumbnail and screwed the bottom of the disposable razor into the top of the can. He pulled up on the razor and it started spinning around like a miniature radar beacon. Natty then gave the side of the can two hard pats, and a faint beeping sound came from within. He set the can down and it continued to beep with the tiny disposable razor spinning above it, sending a constant radio signal.

Natty lay down with his arms behind his head and closed his eyes. He disengaged the two tiny leads hidden in his eyebrows since the continuous electrical current made his eyes tired at times. He removed the glasses, figuring it would be a while before transportation arrived, homing in on his transmitter.

Constantly on the alert since arriving in Libya, Natty was in need of sleep. Within seconds, he was dreaming.

* * *

Careful footsteps brought him fully awake, but his prior training and experience led him to remain motionless; he simply listened. There were two people and they had stopped. He knew they must be shining a light on him and were only a few feet away. Tracker had devised a way to give himself sight again and now had stupidly disengaged it because his eyes were tired. Natty was angry with himself but he forced himself to focus his concentration on the current situation.

Tracker began to move slightly and instantly froze at the sound of two guns being cocked in front of him. His mind registered both sounds: one was a Swedish K rifle, the other a pistol. He knew it was an automatic but couldn't figure out the model. He did know that regardless of type or model, it could shoot holes in him.

The pistol barrel was shoved roughly under his chin, and the gunman grabbed his hair and pulled him to his feet, removing any chance of his replacing the OPTIC and SOD Systems. Natty was now a blind man facing two armed enemies. It was hard not to panic, but panic was not Tracker's style.

A voice came out of the darkness, the pistol holder, he thought. The man said in broken English, "We knew when you watch prison we should follow with lights out. You Israeli?"

Tracker thought back to a particular karate class in which his instructor had taught him how to set up and counter a counter-puncher. The tiny Korean master had blindfolded himself and then had each student try to reverse punch him full in the face or anywhere in the torso they chose, provided they waited until he moved first. In that manner, each of them duplicated the actions of a counter-puncher. Natty remembered how he'd

watched his instructor and been amazed as the man
moved toward each opponent and brought his back hand
up in front of him to the top of his head and swept it
downward with a dropping palm block. No matter
where each adversary punched, the punch had been
caught and blocked harmlessly downward. Tracker had
practiced this repeatedly and was surprised to find how
easy it was to pick off a counter-puncher with this technique.

Tracker now thought that if he moved into the
speaker, the man would move the gun toward him to
fire. Being a man of decision, Natty stepped toward the
speaker, brought his right hand up in front of his face,
and swept it downward with a powerful palm block. At
heart level, his block struck the hand with the gun in
it, and Natty stepped in close while his left hand closed
around the other man's hand and squeezed the man's
finger around the trigger guard. The man screamed in
pain.

In a fraction of a second, Tracker deduced that the
pistol holder probably held a flashlight and that if he
got in close, the other man couldn't take a quick shot
at him. He was right. Still trapping the pistol holder's
hand around the butt, he stuck his own index finger
through the trigger guard and swung the gun in the
general direction of the rifle holder. Natty pulled the
trigger as fast as his finger could move, and he moved
the gun in an arc while he fired fourteen rounds.

He heard a body hit the beach, but still he was totally
afraid for the first time in years. Was the man dropping
to the ground to get a shot at him? Was he now aiming
at Natty's heart? Was he just wounded and still capable
of shooting Natty? Tracker didn't know.

The man with the pistol had no control of the shooting, since he was in extreme pain from Natty's wrist-lock and finger-squeeze. Tracker forced the now-empty pistol back into the screaming man's open mouth and swung viciously upward with a left elbow smash that caught the man under the chin and broke most of his teeth on the gun barrel. Natty reached down with his left hand, grabbed the man's groin, and twisted it violently. He then punched him in the face while still holding the pistol. The butt of the automatic demolished the man's facial bones as Natty struck him with all of his might.

Natty dropped to the ground and did a somersault with his heels coming down hard where he figured the rifle-holder's chest would be. Tracker's feet hit sand, and he froze as he heard the man chuckle weakly, death in his voice, both his own and Tracker's. The man sounded to be ten feet away. Tracker stood motionless as the man continued to chuckle. He faced the rifleman and knew by the man's dying laugh that he had no chance.

In very thick English, the rifleman said, "Israeli?"

Tracker stuck his jaw out defiantly, gave the man the finger, and said, "Fuck you!"

Whoosh! Thunk! Wham!

The sounds came almost simultaneously, and Tracker was instantly on the beach, crawling. His hand touched his glasses and he quickly put them on and plugged them in. He also inserted his sonar earpiece.

Sweat poured down his face as he took in the scene. The man who had held the pistol lay on the sand, his face hideously caved in, and he was very dead. The rifleman lay beyond him on his back with a spearfishing harpoon protruding from his forehead. He weighed closed to 250 pounds, Tracker estimated, and appeared to have bullet holes in his neck, chest, left hip, and lower right abdomen. This had been one tough sucker, and Natty was thankful that he hadn't had to fight him hand to hand. On the beach to Tracker's right stood two US Navy SEALs in scuba gear and wet suits.

The one holding the empty speargun said, "Wonder . . ."

And Natty replied, "Woman . . . has big tits."

The SEAL laughed, "Howdy—you were only supposed to respond with the word 'woman.' "

Tracker replied, "Hey, did you ever look at Wonder Woman?"

The SEAL laughed. "Yeah, I see what you mean. Son of a bitch, look what you did to that guy's face, mister."

Tracker said, "Well, I was one dead son of a bitch. I can't tell you how glad I am you guys showed up. Thanks."

"Aw, shit, our pleasure," the SEAL said modestly. "I'm just glad we got some action since our little raft and us had to swim out a torpedo tube to get here. Made me feel like I was a giant sperm cell. Which reminds me. This is Libya. Why don't we jump in our little raft and get the fuck out of here?"

"We can't—yet. These bodies shouldn't be found," Natty said. "We've got to get rid of the bodies and clean up the area."

"No sweat," the SEAL said with his cheerful gravelly voice.

He and his partner ran forward, and each hoisted a body over his shoulder and kicked sand to hide the blood and footprints. One tossed Tracker's bag to him, and he thought a silent "thank you" for his SOD and OPTIC Systems as he caught it. The SEALS jumped in the raft with the bodies and were joined by Tracker, who pushed the rubber craft out into the mild surf. They started rowing and the leader laughed in Natty's direction.

He said, "Hey it's 0400 hours; you can take off yer Foster Grants, you know."

Tracker smiled and yelled above the sound of the waves, "Can't help it. When you guys saved my bacon back there, you just dazzled me with your brilliance. . . . Shhh!" Tracker whispered, "Don't move— a boat's coming."

The head SEAL whispered, "Probably the sub. No sweat."

Natty replied, "No, the sub is still submerged about a mile further out. This one's going to be coming around that point over there. Lay down in the raft."

A minute later, a Libyan patrol boat came around the rocky outcropping and passed by, its spotlight passing a few feet from the bobbing black raft.

After it was gone, the two SEALS rowed faster, and the leader said, "Fuck, was that close. How in the hell did you hear that boat? And how in the hell do you know where the sub is?"

Tracker smiled. "It's simple. I'm just wearing sunglasses to cut down the bright moonlight and starlight. If you guys wore them, you would've seen both boats, too. As a matter of fact, the sub is near the surface now."

Both SEALs turned and a short time later saw the nuclear sub silently break the water's surface.

The previously silent SEAL finally said to the leader, "I finally figured it out, Lieutenant. He's Spiderman."

All three laughed heartily as their tiny craft moved closer to the big submarine.

10.

The War Before the Battle

DR. EDMUND J. Tetrau had a Ph.D. in sociology from Northwestern University. He always wrote his name with the term "Dr." preceding it and the term "Ph.D." following it, and nobody but nobody thought about addressing him as Ed or Eddie. A forty-year-old black man in tweed jackets, forever clenching an old pipe between his teeth, Dr. Tetrau was not only a total slob but a complete asshole as well.

Edmund had been born to a very poor family living in the middle of Harlem. The only decent thing he had ever done in his life was to raise himself out of squalor. The problem, however, was that while he did do that, he never showed any interest in motivating other children to do so. Instead, he chose to pretend he was from big money and tried everything possible to hide his past.

In high school in Harlem, Edmund had been something of a nerd and had been constantly picked on by every bully. In college things hadn't been quite as bad because the bullies there weren't as physical, but nevertheless they had made fun of him and intimidated him with derisive comments and put-downs.

He had wanted to pledge one particular fraternity and nobody had really cared much one way or another, except for one young man who was studying pre-law. That young man, Jimmy Ray Powell, was white and had been born and raised in Spartanburg, South Carolina.

Although Jimmy Ray's great-great-grandfather had been a slave owner, Jimmy Ray's family had been one of the most progressive in the South in improving race relations, starting in the fifties and sixties. Many white people over the years have acted as though they don't have a prejudiced bone in their bodies, but when around other white people, laughed just as hard as the rest if somebody told "nigger" jokes.

Jimmy Ray's family wasn't like that. His father had gotten into more than one fight with other men by telling them that the racist terminology they were using was very offensive to him. Jimmy Ray's mother had once washed his mouth out with soap when he was young for repeating a joke with the term "jungle bunny" in it.

It so happened, however, that Jimmy Ray had caught Edmund trying to copy his test answers in a world lit class they shared. After class, they had words about it, and Jimmy Ray had let Edmund know that he didn't like busting his ass studying all night only to have somebody steal his answers. Jimmy Ray had never told anyone, though; he had kept it between Edmund and himself. Then later, Edmund had become furious when he learned that Jimmy Ray was president of the fraternity he wanted to join and was blocking him from pledging.

Edmund had at first been very angry and vocal, but

finally had acted as though the matter were dropped. In actuality, he had been busy behind the scenes. One of the professors at the school who was black had been a very passionate civil rights activist, and a personal friend of Dr. Martin Luther King Jr.

Edmund had gone to this man privately and told him that their conversation and knowledge of each other had to be kept totally confidential since Edmund was frightened for his life. Edmund put on a very convincing act as he told the professor a complete fabrication about his trying to join the fraternity, and that Jimmy Ray was trying to block his joining. He stated that many fraternity members wanted him to join because of his popularity, which was too much for the bigotted southerner to endure.

Edmund claimed that he had been walking across campus one night after closing the library while studying for a world lit exam, and he had been dragged into the bushes by three men in sheets and white hoods. He added that the spokesman had a voice and accent identical to Jimmy Ray's.

Edmund claimed that Jimmy Ray had said, "Boy, we don't want no more dirty fucking niggers in our fraternity, and if you don't keep away, you'll be picking cotton on the bottom of Lake Michigan."

Edmund was a convincing liar; the professor had been totally outraged. First, he checked quietly with a couple of students that he knew and trusted in the fraternity and learned that Jimmy Ray had, in fact, been very vocal in his opposition to Edmund's pledging. That had seemed to confirm Edmund's story, and it dovetailed with the professor's own prejudices about southern whites. It wasn't long before Edmund was pledging the fraternity, and Jimmy Ray, trying desperately to find out why his scholarship had been withdrawn, was back in Spartanburg puzzled as to why life was so unfair.

That had been Dr. Tetrau's first successful effort to advance himself by lying and back-stabbing. It did not bother his conscience at all. In fact, he rather pictured himself a tough enemy for anyone who crossed him. The main problem with his convoluted thinking, however, was that anyone—even Mother Theresa—who had what he wanted, was considered the enemy. By the age of forty, the good doctor had become adept at disposing of his enemies and even practiced his back-stabbing against people who weren't really in his way.

His practices had, thus far, gotten him to a GS-15 administrative position with the CIA. Starting out as an Intelligence Analyst, his career had been varied with the agency. Once he had to go out in the field to keep tabs on an upcoming coup attempt in a small African country, but not wanting to be close to any kind of shooting, he had manipulated his way the hell out of there, thank you very much.

Dr. Edmund Tetrau knew something was up with Natty Tracker, the tall, good-looking blind son of a bitch many of the women at the agency sighed over like he was Mel Gibson or Patrick Swayze. He had been in briefings with Tracker and had heard stories about his working directly for the President under the direction of Wally Rampart, whom Edmund hated bitterly.

Rampart was everything Edmund was not; honest, straightforward, hard-working, and incorruptible. Edmund had not yet tried to stick any of his invisible knives in Wally's back, primarily because he was scared to death of him. The fear did not, however, outweigh Edmund's pride in his ability to get whomever he set his sights on.

* * *

Two days had passed since Tracker's extraction from Libya, and he sat in an apartment in the American community in Dharhan, Saudi Arabia. The "safehouse" was a furnished apartment supposedly maintained for executives visiting ARAMCO Oil's headquarters in Dharhan, but was actually used by US, British, and Israeli intelligence operatives. Tracker had been joined by Wally Rampart, and the general didn't know why the mission had been put on hold either. But like Tracker, he knew that Peter Roberts' captivity and torture at the hands of The Ratel would soon end. But both of them also knew every hour would seem like two eternities for the tormented pilot.

Dr. Edmund Tetrau had gone discreetly to the Secretary of State and told him that the CIA had a critical Top Secret operation that he could not explain because the Secretary really wouldn't want to know in case he were ever questioned by Congress. After considering what Ollie North and John Poindexter had gone through, the Secretary had agreed.

Edmund explained that Tracker's mission, whatever it was, had to be temporarily halted or many covert CIA agents and agent handlers in the Mideast would be exposed and most would be killed. Edmund had reemphasized the fact that the mission and his conversation with the Secretary were classified Top Secret, and was only on a need-to-know basis. Consequently, Wally Rampart had been given the order by the Secretary of State to halt the mission, no questions asked, until he gave him further word. Wally was authorized to talk directly to the President, but the President was in the midst of a number of closed-door meetings about secret developments in his war on drugs and had left very firm word that he was not to be disturbed unless World War III broke out.

"I can't go in after Rabbit without backup," Natty said disgustedly.

"I know," Wally replied. "I can't figure out why the hell they've put us on hold. We've got to find out somehow."

"General, can you commandeer a Navy F-14 Tomcat?" Tracker asked.

"Sure, but why?"

"Tomcat's are two-seaters . . . I can fly it and you can be the guy in the back," Tracker replied.

"You can fly it?" Rampart said, astounded. "Besides that, doesn't the navigator have to fly in the back seat?"

Tracker laughed uproariously. "What the hell do we need a navigator for? I'm totally blind, remember?"

Wally, roaring with laughter himself, clapped a beefy hand on Natty's shoulder and said, "I guess you're right, Tracker. Well, what the fuck? Let's get going."

Wally Rampart, hero of countless skirmishes and battles, sweated bullets while the G-forces pinned him against the back seat of the Navy F-14 Tomcat as it raced down the deck of the USS *Nimitz* and screamed skyward, an unsighted pilot at the controls.

In Washington, Natty and Wally drove directly to the home of the Secretary of State and got him out of bed at 4:30 A.M. Tracker was amazed at the demeanor of the Secretary's unflappable wife. Dutifully, she came out of a deep sleep and cheerfully prepared and served the three men coffee.

Over the steaming brew served in Noritake china,

Wally and Tracker pled their case for the next hour until Dr. Edmund Tetrau arrived.

Pulling up in a small BMW, Tetrau was visibly shaken when he emerged from the car. He could feel his pulse pounding in his neck. Diarrhea pangs made him want to run to the bathroom, and he was sick to his stomach. At the kitchen table, he had to concentrate all his energies to keep his hand from shaking while he drank coffee.

"Dr. Tetrau," the Secretary said, "you mentioned a Top Secret operation being compromised if Tracker's mission isn't halted. What is it?"

Wiping sweat from his upper lip, Tetrau answered, "Mr. Secretary, you know that classified information is only supposed to be divulged on a need-to-know basis. I simply—"

Wally interrupted, "Listen, you back-stabbing wimp, why the hell are you trying to disrupt our operation?"

The Secretary of State put his palm up to Wally and said, "General Rampart, you're in my house. I'll thank you to let me handle this."

Wally didn't say a word; he brooded and sipped his coffee.

The Secretary led Edmund to a pair of double hand-carved oak doors and showed him through. Tracker pictured a massive library with a fireplace and overstuffed leather chairs. Before closing the large doors, the balding Secretary of State looked at Wally and gave him a wink and a smile.

Within the rustic library, the Secretary offered Edmund a seat and poured him a snifter of brandy. The doctor thanked him and sat back, finally relaxing slightly.

Smiling as only a politician can, the Secretary said

calmly, "Dr. Tetrau, I'd like to apologize for the remarks made by Undersecretary Rampart. He was totally out of line."

Brushing the remark aside, Edmund, half gloating, said, "Think nothing of it, Mr. Secretary. I've heard all about General Rampart and his goals."

"His goals?" the Secretary said. "What do you mean, 'his goals'?"

Edmund laughed and shook his finger. "Now, sir, you know that I'm not going to say anything about General Rampart behind his back. Besides, I know that you've heard all about him."

"Heard what, Doctor? It's okay. You may speak freely."

Edmund lit his pipe and said, "Oh, Mr. Secretary, I really don't want to say anything, but I'm sure you know that Undersecretary Rampart has designs on your job, and he tries to operate behind your back quite often. I wouldn't say anything like this if I wasn't quite certain that you are already aware of this situation."

"Of course, Doctor," the Secretary said, as he paced around the library deep in thought, "but I *wasn't* aware, and I certainly appreciate you warning me."

Edmund was now gloating. "Don't mention it, sir. We who are loyal to the President and support his programs have to watch each other's backs. This is certainly a town of politics, is it not?"

The Secretary beamed, "It certainly is, Dr. Tetrau, and I appreciate your concern. It's nice to know there are some friends out there. Tell me, the Top Secret operation that would have been compromised, did you actually make that up to cover me?"

Smiling, Dr. Edmund Tetrau cocked his eyebrow, poured himself another snifter of brandy, raised it to the Secretary and replied, "Well, yes. I suspected that the operation they were working on was something cooked up behind your back, so I wanted to halt it until you were able to sort the whole mess out."

The Secretary stood directly in front of Edmund's chair, looking down at the now-uncomfortable spy.

He said calmly, "Dr. Tetrau, I want to tell you something about Wally Rampart. He was eating supper two months ago in a downtown restaurant and saw my twenty-five-year-old daughter eating dinner with a very well-known cocaine dealer. He doesn't know that I know about this.

"She saw him, but he tried to scoot out of the restaurant before she could spot him, not knowing she had. My daughter had only met Wally one time, but the following day, she and her fellow narcotics officers arrested her date, and the man wanted to know if Wally was her father.

"You see, Wally followed both of them until my daughter was safely home, and then he grabbed the dealer and beat the shit out of him. He told the man he'd be tortured and murdered if he was seen within two hundred yards of my daughter again.

"Wally didn't know that my daughter was a narcotics agent. He just thought she was in trouble, and he's never mentioned a breath of it to me or my daughter.

"Now that's the man you're trying to slander.

"I want to make myself very clear. I know all about you, Tetrau. You're a back-stabbing little worm. Somehow, you made it to GS-15, but you're playing with the big boys now, and quite frankly you aren't smart enough to carry our water bucket.

"I'll give you two choices. One is that you turn in a letter of resignation within thirty days, or two, if you don't, I guarantee you that 31 days from today, you'll be standing in the Oval Office getting personally dressed down and booted out of this town by the President of the United States. Which option do you choose?''

Tetrau jumped up and sputtered, ''Now see here, Mr. Secretary, you can't—''

The Secretary interrupted, ''Dr. Tetrau, there will be no arguing or further discussion. You have only two options; which do you choose?''

Walking to the door, head down, Tetrau said softly, ''I'll resign.''

''Fine, fine,'' the Secretary responded cheerfully. ''Glad to hear it. You know the way out. Good-bye.''

Edmund slammed the door and brushed past Wally and Natty without looking at either one. Out on the Secretary's front lawn, he wheeled around and flipped the finger to the house. He drove away thinking of remarks he wished he'd made.

The Secretary of State emerged from his library wearing a bemused grin, lighting a cheroot.

Motioning with his index finger, he said, ''General Rampart, if I could speak with you for one minute.''

Wally raised his palm and said, ''Mr. Secretary, it's not necessary. I was way out of line. I totally fucked up and I apologize.''

The Secretary just grinned, puffed on his cigar, and said, ''Okay. Now if Mr. Tracker's going to get in there and save his old buddy, you'd better get back to the Mideast, pronto. Do you have fast transportation?''

Wally and Natty looked at each other, grinning broadly, and Wally said, ''Yes, we do. We borrowed an F-14 to get here. I suppose we'd better return it.''

The Secretary laughed and replied, ''That, or answer for the President when Sam Donaldson asks him why the Navy lost an expensive jet. Call for a refueler to meet you in the air, and as far as that goes, anything you need to accomplish your mission is yours, Mr. Tracker. Believe me, I'm speaking on behalf of the Secretary of Defense and the President. You two better make tracks.''

Beaming, both warriors waved, nodded, and headed for the door but were stopped by the diplomat's summons. They looked at him with appreciation.

The Secretary said, ''Good luck, Tracker.''

Wally replied before Natty had a chance, ''Thanks Mr. Secretary. Tracker makes his own luck.''

By noon of the following day, Edmund Tetrau knew the essence of Tracker's mission by simply manipulating several secretaries and assistants in Wally's office. A crooked smile played on his lips as he dialed the telephone.

Somebody had apparently answered and Edmund said, ''Yes, hello, I'm sorry, I didn't hear you. Is this the *National Tattler*? . . . Yes, I'd like to speak to your international affairs correspondent, please. Frank Richmond is it? . . . Oh, I uh, have a very hot news item for him . . . My name? Oh, I can't tell that. Just tell him that I'm a high-ranking executive in the State Department . . . Yes, that will be fine, I'll wait. Thank you.''

11.

The Insertion

THE US AIR Force C-130 Hercules shuddered with exertion as the little jets on its sides flamed out, trying to help the four mighty engines, and whirring propellers labored to lift the giant cargo plane off the runway at Catania, Sicily. It was suddenly airborne and roared into the moonless sky carrying its Top Secret cargo southward toward the land of Wacky Qaddafi.

A half-hour later, the tailgate opened and the camouflage-painted bird excreted its contents into the Mediterranean night sky. As the mighty C-130 banked and loudly throbbed off into the darkness, the contents of its steel bowels fell silently toward the blue sea thousands of feet below. Inside those contents, Natty Tracker pulled a lever that released several clamps. Heavy duty spring-loaded hinges went into action, a pair of wings unfolded twice, and the big glider soared silently southward toward the distant shoreline of Libya.

Natty banked and climbed, searching for thermals to help him stay aloft a little longer as he glided noiselessly southward toward a rendezvous with destiny. He had not "soared" since his younger days at the Air

Force Academy, and he was enjoying it. He remembered being towed in front of the Rampart Range by a single-engine plane and turned loose. He had sailed in circles and looked over at nearby Pike's Peak and east at the massive prairie. Northward, he could see the busy metropolis of Denver. On several of those days, he had spotted jets from units visiting Petersen Air Force Base, "Pete Field" as the locals called it. The jets, usually in pairs, attacked mock targets at Fort Carson's ordnance impact area. Watching those jets, Tracker had dreamed of the independence of pushing himself and one of those awesome weapons to the limit. He had imagined passing through corridors of space like a Perregrine falcon streaking after its prey.

Natty had followed one short-term goal after another, and seemingly "in the blink of an eye" he was one of those fighter pilots he'd dreamed about becoming. His whole life had been like that. Tracker set goals for himself, some big, some small, and then went after them. Whatever else happened on the way was inconsequential.

Natty thought of Fancy Bird and wondered what she was doing. He pictured her perfect body. Like Natty, she was very athletic and had learned she had to work out with regularity to maintain both her physical and mental well-being. He thought about her eyes and the playfulness he'd spotted in them the first time they met. Tracker had that tiny signal in his own eyes, and he looked for it in women. Her legs were long with very tanned calves and thighs. Her ankles were slim and her feet delicate. Her stomach was about as flat as a woman's could be, but her buttocks were well rounded. Her breasts were very firm and large. Her face, he thought, reminded him of Marilyn Monroe's with a different hair color and complexion. Natty promised himself that he'd take her on a vacation to Bora Bora as soon as this mission was finished.

He saw the sandy shoreline.

Tracker pushed a button on the cockpit display in front of him and a female computer voice said in an electronic monotone, "Altitude: 6,000 feet. Speed: seven-zero knots."

Natty whistled the theme from *The Magnificent Seven* while he unbuckled his safety harness, twisted around, and pulled an aviator kit bag from behind the seat. It had a fifteen-foot canvas tether that he hooked to the webbing of his parachute harness. Next, he tied the bag just below the emergency parachute on his abdomen with a quick-release knot. He yanked two levers, and the canopy above him popped open, the wind stripping it away from the aircraft. He put the glider into a slight dive while he turned to starboard and nosed it into a climb.

When the plane slowed drastically, he leveled it off, bunched his knees under his muscular torso, and leaped straight up. The sailplane went into an immediate dive while Natty steadied his body into a stable freefall. It felt as if he were suspended in midair instead of dropping toward the ocean at 120 miles per hour. At one-hundred-foot intervals, a barometrically triggered computer voice, in the same electronic nasal tone, announced the altitude. At thirteen hundred feet Natty grabbed the ring on the left side of his harness and yanked. The little pilot chute popped open above his back and pulled out a large black parachute. With only a glance at the canopy to insure it was fully blossomed, Natty checked the toggle lines and risers with his fingers to make sure there were no tangles. His eyes followed the glider, far away now, and he watched as it plunged into the Mediterranean.

He pulled the quick-release knot on the tether line, and the heavy aviator kit bag dropped below, its swinging making Natty look like the apex of a pendulum. He pulled on his toggles and steered the chute into the swing, steadying it. Next, he pushed a button on his harness and there was a pop and a hissing sound below as a tube inflated around the base of the aviator kit bag.

Tracker looked down, squeezed the frame of his glasses, and his vision zoomed into a close-up look at the bag. Assured that the flotation ring had functioned properly, he released the frame and his field of vision returned to normal. This zoom lens feature was a new option Tracker had added to the OPTIC System a month earlier. With his automatic night vision capability, he was looking at everything around him with almost the same clarity afforded by daylight.

Natty looked down at the blue waters that seemed to be rising rapidly to meet him. He reached across his chest and grabbed the upper right webbing of his parachute harness with his left hand. With his right hand, he pulled a steel safety clip on a yellow line. Then he twisted the large quick-release on the front of his harness. The aviator kit bag hit the water, and Tracker hit the quick-release plate on his chest. The four main sections of his canvas harness snapped loose, and he quickly raised his arms overhead and slipped into the water.

The parachute, like the glider, had been made to sink to the ocean's depths, and it was soon out of sight beneath the surface. Tracker swam to the kit bag, opened it, and pulled out an underwater rebreathing apparatus that he strapped on his back. He took out a diving mask,

dipped it in the water, spat on the faceplate, wiped the
spittle around to prevent fogging, and donned the mask.
He put on a pair of flippers, pulled out a small pack
that he strapped to his chest, and yanked the ripcord
on the kit bag's seam. The air hissed out of the flotation
ring and the bag sank. Natty put his mouthpiece in,
took a few breaths, and disappeared into the warm sea,
his fins sticking out with one final wave to the fresh
air.

The Ratel couldn't sleep, but that wasn't uncommon,
so he walked down the hall and told the guard to awaken
the sleeping imperialist pilot. The Ratel would enter-
tain himself by hearing Captain Roberts scream again.

Pedro had a recurring dream. In it, he was in a fierce
battle against enemies carrying all types of weapons,
both primitive and modern. He held only a knife but
was dispatching his foes, who all looked like himself,
and were piling up around him. Finally, one man, the
comic book character Sergeant Rock, came at him,
grinning. Pedro, drenched in sweat and blood, stabbed
him over and over again. He saw the knife go into Sergeant Rock's torso, face, and neck, but it bounced out
without leaving a hole or any blood. The American GI
just grinned, a thick cigar clenched between his teeth.

Sergeant Rock laughed and said, "I'm gonna make
a steer outta you, boy."

In a blind rage now, The Ratel stabbed him faster
and more furiously but to no avail. The GI just kept
coming.

Finally, soaked in perspiration and almost hyperven-
tilating, he woke up, often with a scream.

Rabbit Roberts was dragged into the room, absolute
fear in his black-lidded eyes. They were sunken now,

and he looked extremely gaunt. His eyebrows were gone, replaced by a series of ugly cigarette burns. With a nod from The Ratel, the guard tied Rabbit's wrist to two rings suspended from the ceiling of the interrogation room. His ankles were then tied to two rings embedded in the floor and his pants yanked down around his ankles. His testicles were swollen and covered with bruises and burns.

Rabbit flinched in near hysteria as the guard splashed water on his groin, but he tried hard to be brave. He panted heavily and gritted his teeth as The Ratel carried an eight-volt car battery over and attached jumper cables to his testicles and then attached the negative pole to the battery and tapped the positive pole with the other cable. Rabbit's body jerked with the jolts of electricity, and he screamed at the top of his lungs.

The Ratel snarled, "Yankee, you have a beeg hero, amigo, who's on hees way to save you."

He laughed with a deep roaring guffaw.

Pedro continued, "He ees totally blind and he ees going to come here and save you. He theenks."

With that, he laughed with greater glee. The Ratel didn't know he'd made a big mistake. Rabbit was at the breaking point, he was ready to give in, tell him what he wanted, and take a quick bullet "between the running lights." He didn't show the monster anything on his face, but The Ratel had let him know that Natty was coming to save him. Blind or not, there was no man Peter would have wanted more on his rescue mission. He felt hope again. He pretended to faint; it had worked once before.

Head down and eyes closed, Rabbit felt a twinge when he heard The Ratel say, "When your savior comes, gringo, we weell have a surprise waiting for heem. Maybe your blind savior weell get crucified, huh, and we weell see eef he ees resurrected.''

The desert sun beat down on the olive grove in which Natty lay hidden. A light sand-colored tarp camouflaged him from all observation as he lay sleeping among the symmetrical rows of olive trees. Not far away his diving gear lay buried deep below the Libyan sand.

As ordered, Mohammad had dropped off an old Volkswagon beetle near the edge of the olive grove.

The Libyan had had little trouble smuggling a package into the country from Egypt by hiding it in his cousin's tired old fishing boat. That package was locked in the trunk in the front of the bug, and the keys had been left atop the left rear tire.

In Athens, Wally Rampart stood in front of a large computer screen.

He said to the CIA computer operator in front of him, ''Okay, program in the letters T-R-C-K-R, then back-slash, then W-K-U-P.''

She did so and hit the key marked ENTER, and miles away, under a small camouflaged tarpaulin, Natty's Tracker's SOD device beeped in his ear. Natty's eyes opened but he didn't move. His senses immediately alert, he shook his head and the beeper stopped. Then he carefully peeked out from under the tarp, decided that the coast was clear, and crawled out. Folding the lightweight nylon tarp and storing it in his hip pocket, Natty stood next to an olive tree and checked out his surroundings more thoroughly. The old VW was parked under the setting desert sun and Tracker carefully made his way to it.

Natty retreived the keys and opened the trunk, removed the package, and opened it, grinning at the contents. He pulled out a pair of MAC-11 machine pistols and four loaded magazines mounted in twin leather shoulder holsters. He donned the shoulder harness over the desert-tan jumpsuit he wore.

The back of the harness contained a tube-shaped holster that held a pair of octagonal oak nunchaku, better known as "karate sticks," "nunchucks," or just plain "chucks." Made famous by the actor Bruce Lee in the movie *Enter the Dragon*, the nunchaku is a pair of wooden sticks, a foot long and an inch thick, connected by a small chain, with ball bearing swivels at the end of each stick.

Originally, the nunchaku were tools used by Okinawan farmers for threshing rice. When Okinawa was occupied by Japan, the natives were forbidden to own weapons, so they learned how to use their farm implements as weapons against raping, pillaging samurai warriors. When used for striking, the outer stick of the nunchucks travels at five times the speed of the inner stick and is capable of smashing a brick. They are used to block weapons and fists, for choke holds, and bone-crunching locking techniques.

Natty donned a drab *baraccan*, the traditional dress of the Libyan male. He carefully placed the box back in the little car and drove off toward nearby Tripoli.

At nightfall, he parked the German car and removed the *baraccan* after retrieving the backpack from the package. He put it on so it fit neatly over his shoulder harness. Tracker then took off into the darkness for the prison where his friend was being tortured.

Within an hour, Tracker was in sight of the massive fortress prison, but he was still beyond the reach of its searchlights. Reaching into his backpack that he'd set before him, he pulled out an electronic control box with a series of buttons, gauges, and a large toggle stick on it. He next pulled out what looked to be a model aircraft. Within three minutes a four-foot-long replica of the army's deadly Apache assault helicopter sat on the desert sand in front of him. Natty opened the gas line and hooked a small wire over the nylon rotor blade. He spun the blade in the opposite direction from the way it normally spins and released it. The tension from the spring wire spun the seven-foot-long rotors, and the engine whirred into action with a surprisingly quiet hum.

Tracker pulled a pin from a cover on the control board and lifted the red flap up. A red display blinked; it read: WARNING: ARMED. He looked at the three other buttons labeled MISSILE, CANNON, SELF-DESTRUCT. He put the backpack on, picked up the control board, and moved stealthily toward the prison. One hundred yards out, he stopped, lay down on the still-hot sand, and placed the board directly in front of him.

He looked at the armed guards on the wall and in the towers and grabbed the controls. The helicopter lifted off, zoomed over Tracker, and headed toward the high block wall. None of the guards heard the relatively quiet engine until the miniature chopper was twenty yards away, but by then, it was too late.

Aiming the mini-Apache at the closest tower, Tracker pushed the cannon button and there was a staccato clicking sound as the electronically controlled Gatling gun, powered by a powerful compressed air cylinder, spouted out brass pellets at a rate of 3,600 per minute. Dropping the closest tower guard, it swept along the wall, armed but stunned guards falling every few seconds. Each of them was literally shredded by the intense firepower, but not one actually knew what hit him.

Tracker swept the other walls, wiping out guards, then swooped toward the farthest tower guard who was now trying to aim at the miniature aircraft. He pushed the missile button and one of two small missiles fired and exploded inside the tower with the force of a standard high explosive hand grenade.

Natty flew the chopper toward the other back tower, but the guard dropped out of sight. Tracker maneuvered the helicopter into the tower and pushed the self-destruct button. The aircraft exploded along with the guard's head. Two seconds later, two thermite charges built into the control board detonated, and the mechanism burned itself up from the inside out.

Natty took off at a dead run toward the prison, and hosed down the last tower guard with a burst of fire from his right-hand MAC-11. He had buried his backpack and was carrying what appeared to be a leather briefcase. It was actually a device stuntmen use called an Air-Ram, and Tracker dropped it at the base of the wall less than half a minute after the attack had begun. He pushed a button and the compressed air-powered device exploded, propelling Natty upward. He grabbed the edge of the wall and pulled himself up. He hung on the lip of the wall, affixed a small grappling hook connected by thin steel cable to a reel inside his shirt on the edge, and dropped to the ground inside the prison.

Tracker had examined satellite photos of the penitentiary with Wally Rampart and knew immediately which door to head for. Reaching the big wooden steel-barred door, he put a small penlike device inside the big lock. Natty pushed a button on his watch and ducked back as the small bomb exploded inside the lock. Natty ran forward and pushed the massive smoking door open. Inside, there was a small office to the left and a rock-hewn stairway winding down to his right. Natty bounded down the steps and into a pitch black room.

He immediately knew he'd walked into a trap. The Ratel didn't know Tracker could see in the dark nearly as well as a sighted person could in the daylight. In an instant, Tracker saw that The Ratel had his hand on a light switch and was about to flip it on. He also saw ten armed guards in the room along with a newspaper taped up all over the walls. It was the front page of the *National Tattler* and the headline read: TATTLER EXCLUSIVE! BLINDED PILOT ON HEROIC TOP SECRET RESCUE MISSION.

Before anyone realized what was happening, Tracker lunged forward and broke Pedro's left hand by the light switch with a quick downswing of his nunchucks. Not stopping, he swept around the darkened room flailing left and right. Within seconds, he had incapacitated six of the guards, and he swung both pistols up as The Ratel reached the switch with his right hand and turned the lights on.

Then there was blackness.

Fancy Bird and Wanda Leigh were both naked and writhing on both sides of his body. He'd scarcely made up his mind which one to kiss when the other searched for his hungry mouth with hers. Both were stroking his face, but with the other hand, they took turns hitting him on the back of the head with wooden mallets. Wait, he thought, this doesn't make sense. I'm dreaming.

"No, you aren't," Wanda said and struck him again with the mallet.

Tracker awakened. Sitting up quickly with a moan,

he reached up and rubbed a nasty lump on the back of his head and eyed his surroundings. Natty was in a stone cell in the basement of the prison. He still had his OPTIC and SOD Systems. His lightweight tarp was the only thing that hadn't been taken from his pockets. He quickly dug a hole in the sand floor and hid it.

No sooner had he done this than his door opened and two guards walked in with a third covering him with his own MAC-11. Tracker was led down a long hot hallway with a high barred window. The passageway had a sandy floor, and he made mental notes on all of it. Natty was led up a few steps and through a door into a stone-floored room. He looked up into the blazing eyes of The Ratel. They seated him at a thick wooden table, and his hands were strapped down as his legs were cuffed to the chair legs. The Ratel, a sadistic leer on his scarred face, reached behind his neck, and pulled out a large curved dagger, and stuck it into the table.

He said, "What are America's plans for Leebya?"

Natty grinned and said, "Eat shit and die."

The package had been carried to Wally Rampart by special diplomatic courier. It had been addressed to the President and dropped off at the American Embassy in Tel Aviv by a little boy who ran off into a crowd nearby. It was signed, "The Ratel."

Attached was a note to Wally from the top local CIA agent telling Wally that the package had been checked for explosives. With that in mind, the old general opened the package and stared down into the box, his eyes narrowing to slits. He jumped up, clenching his teeth, and slammed a beefy fist on the table in the embassy conference room. The box fell on its side, and a finger rolled out. On the front of the tanned digit, between the knuckle and first joint was a white scar in the shape of a capital T.

12.

Out of the Jaws

NATTY EXAMINED THE stump of his left ring finger where The Ratel had slowly sawed it off below the knuckle. He'd made a tourniquet from threads in his jumpsuit and used a swatch from it to make a pressure bandage.

Following the example of his forefathers, Tracker had stared into Pedro's eyes while the psychopath sawed his finger off, and he had shown no emotion, not one wince of pain. The little boy inside of him had wanted to scream and cry, but Tracker had too much self-discipline.

The amputation was now very painful, but Natty knew he'd handle it. He was thankful that The Ratel had allowed him to keep his glasses, saying he wanted Tracker to watch while his own intestines were pulled out of his body. Tracker had simply grinned at Pedro and calmly informed him that, even with his intestines removed, he would still kill him with his bare hands. For that reason alone, he was glad he still had nine other fingers.

Natty's thoughts returned to his mission. He had

come here to find and rescue Rabbit, and he was single-minded in his pursuit of that goal. With that in mind, Tracker removed a shoe and tapped on each wall of his cell with the heel. He heard a faint tapping of Morse code through the south wall of the cell. He listened to the tapping and interpreted it: R-B-T. It was Rabbit. He tapped back: T-R-K-R. For the rest of the day, the two sent messages back and forth telling the extent of each other's injuries. Tracker also learned who had the keys, a guard Rabbit called Yogi. This made Tracker chuckle, as it aptly described the man who looked like Yogi Bear.

The following morning, three guards again came to get Tracker. One of them was Yogi. He was taken to the interrogation room and tied by his wrists to the ceiling and by his ankles to the floor. The Ratel entered the room, his left hand sporting a cast from Natty's blow with the nunchucks. Tracker had been in too much pain from the previous meeting to notice it, but this time he commented on it.

He said, "What happened, Pedro? Did your mother grow teeth in her pussy?"

The Ratel stared at Natty with absolute hate in his eyes, but his hatred had nothing to do with the insult. There was something about this tall dark American Pedro feared. Tracker was blind, sort of. He was unarmed and under guard, and The Ratel was considered one of the most, if not *the* most, dangerous men in the world, but for some reason, Tracker seemed to hold the upper hand.

When Pedro had cut off Tracker's finger, the American hadn't flickered an eyelid.

Instead, he had grinned and said, "Oh, are we having finger sandwiches for lunch my first day here? I hope you don't plan to serve foot-long hot dogs anytime soon.''

Perhaps it was this fear that had caused him to let Tracker live. Or maybe it was simply because his madman boss said he wanted both Americans alive to sell back to the United States. Even The Ratel didn't trust Colonel Qaddafi's mental stability. Pedro might send the smaller pilot back in one skin, but there was no way he'd let this Tracker live. He had to kill his fear no matter what.

He walked slowly up to the American, knife in hand. He looked at the base of Natty's throat and remembered looking at his own mother's throat years before, when he'd slit it trying to rid himself of his unglorious past. He remembered the look of horror on her face, then an expression of relief just before she died.

He smiled at Tracker and said, "Gringo, you joke now, but tomorrow you weel not laugh as I slowly peel your skeen off and gut you. Every time you faint from thee pain, we weel throw water on you and wake you to feel eet good.''

Tracker laughed and smirked, "I doubt if you could peel an apple without a training course. Even then, if they gave you a five-minute break, they'd have to retrain you.''

No one had ever made fun of Pedro before. He had always been treated with deference, if not abject fear. The hideous scar on his face turned beet red as it always did when The Ratel was wrankled. He had to pay Tracker back somehow, with something worse than mere physical pain.

He said, "Amigo, een a few days, when your carcass ees already rotteeng, your Presidente ees going to vee-seet Israel. Do you know what wee weel do?''

"What?" Tracker responded, trying to act disinterested.

The Ratel was angered because Tracker didn't seem alarmed.

He continued, "Wee weel have some men who weel be een the uniforms of the Israeli Army, and they weel open fire on your Presidente. They are goeeng to sacreefice their lives for Leebya. Eesn't that stupid, sacreeficeeng their lives for thees beeg pile of sand?"

"Oh, I don't know," Tracker replied, "you made that decision."

"What deceesion?" The Ratel said angrily.

"To die for this big pile of sand, Pedro," Tracker said with a big grin. "And this isn't even your country. To me, that's really stupid."

"Someday, maybe a bullet weel take me, Tracker, but not from you," Pedro hissed, beads of sweat popping out on his face. "Tomorrow, first theeng, you weel feel thee blade of my knife as eet slowly peels your skeen away from thee flesh. Then we weel see how brave thee mighty Tracker ees."

Tracker said nonchalantly, "Hate to disappoint you, but you won't die from a bullet."

Pedro looked at Natty quizzically.

Tracker said, "I'm going to cut your left ring finger off and force it down your throat and let you choke on it until you turn blue and die."

It took all The Ratel's self-control to hide the cold chill that passed through his body and the wave of nausea that gripped his intestines. He stepped forward and opened the top of Natty's jumpsuit. He dug the blade of his knife into Tracker's upper chest and dragged it down Natty's muscular torso. Again, Tracker didn't flinch.

Pedro spoke after licking Tracker's blood off of his fingers, "You seem to forget who ees thee preesoner, Tracker."

Tracker smiled calmly and said, "No, I don't forget that at all. I know who the prisoner is. You created your own cell for yourself years ago, Pedro. You haven't given any loyalty to anyone or anything, so you've gone through all your short life never able to sleep comfortably, never able to trust anyone. People only feel hate or fear toward you, and lots of people will breathe easier once you've been killed, so now I'll do it for them."

"Why do you speak like thees?" The Ratel raged. "Perhaps I weel keel you now, huh?"

Tracker said evenly, "No, you'll wait, hoping that I'll become afraid, and that'll diminish your fear of me somewhat. The only problem is that you'll never see fear from me, Pedro. But you *will* see death."

Pedro felt a chill grip his very soul, but he hid it and snarled, "Tomorrow, amigo, we weel see who peeses on whose dead body."

The Ratel turned and stormed out of the room.

Yogi and the other two guards came in to take Tracker back to his cell.

Natty knew that the life of the President of the United States depended on his actions. He had to get away immediately. If Libyans dressed and probably ID'ed as Israeli soldiers shot the President—he shuddered to think of the international political implications.

His attack on the guards had to be quick, silent, and deadly. He would be facing three tough opponents, all killers, and one was pointing a MAC-11 machine pistol at him right now. That was Yogi, the one with the keys; he would die first. The one to Tracker's left was athletic; he would die second. The third was the largest, but he was awkward. He would die last, Tracker decided.

The two held his arms, and Yogi walked directly behind him, gun in hand. Without looking, Tracker suddenly stopped in the sand-floored hallway and dropped to one knee while shoving the two unarmed guards forward and off balance. He drove an elbow smash backward into Yogi's groin as he grabbed the MAC-11 barrel with his left hand. He snapped a backfist flush into Yogi's face and then hammer-fisted him in the groin, doubling him over in pain. He then stood and knee-smashed Yogi's face and came down on the base of his neck with another elbow smash.

The athletic guard aimed a kick at Tracker, but Tracker grabbed the unconscious, falling Yogi by the hair and jerked him into the path of the kick. The heavy Libyan army boot caught Yogi squarely in the face. Tracker snapped a side-kick at the guard's kneecap but just missed. The guard threw a right hand lead at Natty, and Natty swept his right forearm across his face in an inside middle block that caught the guard on the wrist. The guard threw a left at Natty's face, but Natty swept the same arm back across his face in an outside middle block and blocked the punch again at the wrist. He stepped deep past the man's foreleg and swept a crunching ridge-hand with all his strength into the man's nose. The blow broke the guard's nose, cheekbone, and neck.

The largest guard came at him like a bellowing bull, and Natty stepped to the left with a side escape and executed a right spinning hook kick, and the blade of his right foot caved in the bigger man's ribcage. Natty grabbed the stunned 250-pounder and hit him with three powerful right uppercuts into his broken ribs, sending several jagged bones into the lungs. He grabbed the semi-comatose man by the hair and smashed his face into the stone wall.

Tracker retrieved his holsters and weapons from Yogi's body along with the keys. He rushed to Rabbit's cell and opened it. Rabbit had tears in his eyes as he looked at his old friend, and he rushed forward, overcome with emotion, and grabbed Tracker in a bearhug.

Natty hugged his gaunt-looking friend quickly, then stepped back and tossed Rabbit a MAC-11 and whispered, "C'mon, Rabbit, time to head for the Bat-cave!"

The two ran out the door and down the hallway. Yogi wasn't quite dead, so Rabbit stopped to help him along. The two ran up the winding stone steps, Natty running headlong into a hapless guard who got his head caved in by a quick swing from Natty's nunchaku. Tracker found the room that he thought The Ratel stayed in, and he unlocked it and dived inside. The room did not hold his foe, but The Ratel's curved dagger was stuck into a crude wooden table that held some bread and goat meat.

Tracker grabbed the knife and stuck it into his nunchuck holster and, winking at Rabbit, said, "I'll need this later on."

As they opened the two big wooden doors a crack, they saw a Soviet-made 2,000-kilo truck starting to drive out toward the front gate. Keeping it between them and the gate guards, they ran out and dived under the truck, rolled on their backs, and each grabbed part of the axle and lifted their torsos off the ground. Feet dragging in the hot white sand, they passed safely out the gate but were spotted just outside it. Both let go of the axle and opened fire simultaneously, killing the startled guards. There were muffled shouts inside the prison, and a few scattered shots were fired from the walls as they tried to run down the big truck, but the driver pushed the pedal to the metal.

With the gates starting to reopen and sirens blaring, Natty and Rabbit took off across the dunes at a dead run. At last, Natty spotted the Volkswagen, still where he'd parked it behind an old stone building. They were within a stone's throw of the city's outer edge, but they heard vehicles roaring out the gate behind them. There was no way they could make it to the car and they both knew it.

Tracker had grabbed his hidden tarp before escaping and he pulled it out. He threw Rabbit to the ground next to the sandy road and both started digging in the sand. Vehicle engines roaring toward them, they dived into the depression and Natty pulled the sand-colored tarp over them a millisecond before the first of three military landrovers screamed over the top of the dune. The three flew past the hidden duo and entered the outskirts of the city less than one hundred yards away. Tracker and Rabbit crawled out from under the tarp, their eyes following the path of the vehicles.

"Man, that was close," Rabbit said, wiping his brow.

Tracker laughed.

"Close?" he said as he held the tarp up and showed Rabbit the tire tracks running along the edge of it.

Both men took off at a dead run for the old beat-up VW. They were soon barreling down narrow streets with Tracker at the wheel. Both men were thankful it was so hot that most people were indoors trying to escape the unforgiving desert sun.

The inevitable finally happened, however. Some people say that bad luck comes in threes. This happened to the two Americans. While barreling down a long city street, Natty had to slam on the brakes as a landrover filled with six angry soldiers screeched around the corner ahead of them. At the same time, Tracker looked in his rearview mirror and saw a police cruiser with two cops in it slide around the corner behind him. While jamming the floor shift into reverse, Natty heard and then saw a Soviet-made Mi-8 Hip assault helicopter roar overhead, its angry rotors spinning as if searching for an American or two to decapitate. He had just passed a very narrow alley that led at a slight downhill angle all the way to the sea almost two miles distant.

The helicopter fired a burst from its twenty millimeter cannon just as Tracker barreled into the alleyway, his rear bumper torn off by one of the huge rounds. Several seconds later, the helicopter reappeared overhead trying to line up a shot on the fleeing bug. The police cruiser soon followed, siren wailing, with the landrover directly behind it. Both the cruiser and the landrover had a few scant inches on either side of their vehicles to maneuver. The Volkswagen ahead of them was roaring along at top speed sending showers of sparks flying off its fenders as it scraped one wall and then the other.

The confines of the alley were so narrow that one of the cops kicked the windshield out of the cruiser to fire at the fleeing beetle since there was no room to shoot out the side windows.

The helicopter maneuvered into position and fired two rockets. Both missed. It fired again.

Shhh-boom! A miss!

Shhh-boom! Wham! The rubber on the right rear tire exploded into useless pieces of black shrapnel. Sparks showered up from the street as Tracker's car careened on at top speed with just a bare metal rim on its right rear.

The cop saw that the two had ducked down, so he continued to pour shot after shot at the body of the automobile. The cruiser was closing on the wounded little car. The cop started cussing as did the driver when feces and urine splashed in their faces from Natty's tires.

The helicopter lined up on the target again, this time with a computer lock-on. It fired the cannons, and the Volkswagen was killed instantly, its entire body peppered with jagged holes.

Steam poured out the back as the cruiser skidded to a halt behind it. The landrover slammed into the cruiser with such force that the cop with the gun went through the open windshield head first. He was unceremoniously rewarded for his zest and dedication to Wacky Qaddafi by having his head crushed under the front tire of his own cruiser. The driver drew his gun and scrambled out the open windshield and was almost struck from behind by a soldier's bullet. The six soldiers crawled out and everybody dashed forward, guns at the ready.

The cop realized that nobody could have possibly lived through the onslaught from the noisy helicopter now hovering above, all weapons locked on the target. So, making a show of mock bravery, he ran forward and stuck his pistol and head into the blown-out back window of the Volkswagen. He turned and signaled the rest to come and look. They all dashed up and looked in, moaning simultaneously. The accelerator pedal was pushed against the floorboard by Natty's nunchucks wedged against the front of the driver's seat.

One of the soldiers excitedly explained that the only time the Americans could have gotten out was in the few seconds they were out of sight when they had first turned into the narrow alleyway. Several more said they would be long gone before they could get back there and start searching. Two soldiers agreed with the first soldier, the rest disagreed, and they started arguing. It then dawned on the cop that these idiots had killed his partner, and he started screaming at them.

In the meantime, the helicopter pilot and crew hovered overhead wondering how much damage they had wrought with their firepower.

Three-quarters of a mile away, Tracker held his hand over the mouth of a beautiful, struggling Libyan woman. Rabbit nervously watched through a crack in the door of the small two-room stone structure. With Natty's other hand, he held her about the waist, and she sensed that he was only using a fraction of his strength to restrain her. This feeling reassured her to some extent, so she suddenly quit fighting and relaxed. Tracker smiled warmly at her and held his index finger in front of his lips in a shushing manner.

His crystal-clear, powder-blue eyes were riveted on hers, and like most women who fell under their gaze, even through his special dark glasses, the woman melted a bit inside. She caught herself and tried to steady her breathing. She started to move toward a waterbowl in the corner, giving Natty a questioning look.

"Nyet?" she asked meekly.

"Nyet?" Natty said and laughed. "No, no. We aren't Russians. We're Americans."

"American?" she asked, a smile spreading across her face.

"Yes," Natty responded, nodding his head.

He gestured toward the waterbowl and she moved over to it. He walked over to Rabbit as she took a cloth and sponged her face and cleavage. She looked over and saw Tracker's special eyes aimed at her with interest. Embarrassed, she flushed and looked away quickly. Seconds later, however, she glanced at Tracker seductively. He grinned at her.

Pointing to herself, she said, "Fathia."

"Fathia," Tracker replied, "pretty name. I am Tracker."

Showing beautiful white teeth, she smiled and said, "Tracker," with the accent on "ker."

Tracker laughed and shook his head. "No, Tracker, Fathia."

Fathia pronounced it correctly, and when he nodded yes, she said it repeatedly, proud of her newfound knowledge.

Rabbit just shook his head, grinning at Tracker as he said, "Natty, how the hell do you do it? It doesn't matter where in the world we are, you always end up with some beautiful woman saying your name over and over again."

Tracker chuckled, "Hey, I'd rather have her screaming 'Allah!' over and over."

"Oh, bullshit," Rabbit replied. "You and I both know you'll have her doing it before we get out of here."

Tracker smiled, "Well, I *do* think we ought to hide out here until dark. Don't you agree?"

"Tracker, would it really matter if I didn't? I just want to know how you do it."

Tracker grinned impishly and replied innocently,

"Gosh, I don't know, Peter. I don't say anything to them. All I do is stand there and lick my eyebrows."

Rabbit started laughing. Because this was the first chance for his pent-up nervous system to unwind, he kept laughing, nearly to the point of hysteria. Understanding the universal language of laughter, Fathia started laughing too, as did Tracker. Rabbit slid down the wall and soon all three were on the floor, tears rolling down their cheeks.

They finally regained their composures, and Natty stood and helped Fathia off the floor. He stared deep into her eyes and lightly touched her soft cheek with the back of his bronze hand.

"First or second watch?" Tracker asked Peter.

"Go ahead, you son of a bitch," Rabbit replied. "I'll take first watch while you get your knob polished."

Tracker grinned at his friend.

He said with mock seriousness, "I need it polished, Rabbit, if we're to open the door between the Arab world and the West. I like to dive into international relations headfirst."

"I bet you do," Rabbit said with a smirk.

Tracker smiled down at Fathia and took her by the hand. She allowed herself to be led into the adjoining room. She examined his amputation, and he calmly slid her simple dress off her shoulders and let it fall to the floor. She looked up into his glasses, trying to imagine his entrancing eyes, and reached out and unzipped his jumpsuit. She pulled it off his broad shoulders and removed it, marveling at Natty's muscular body and shocked at the fresh knife wound down his chest. Words were not needed as the two strangers made slow, passionate love long into the afternoon.

* * *

Tracker was on watch when they came, just two hours before nightfall. They came suddenly from around the corner and prepared to kick in the door. The search party consisted of six members of the Libyan army, and they were not enthusiastic to execute a house-to-house search for the two Imperialist escapees, who were reported to have been broken out of prison by a superior force of heavily armed American mercenaries. Natty had only enough time to give Rabbit, who was napping in the other room, a whistle and to shove Fathia into a corner.

Rabbit appeared in the doorway, MAC-11 in hand, and Natty signaled him to drop. Then Tracker stooped down by the open window. The door opened with a crash and three soldiers ran into the room as Natty dived headfirst out the open window.

Executing a somersault in midair, Tracker fired while still upside down and kept shooting after he hit the ground, killing the three soldiers who were still outside the door. He ran to the door, while Rabbit opened fire on the other three inside. Two of them went down, and the third was firing at Rabbit when Tracker charged in the door, drawing the man's attention. A quick burst from Rabbit sent him to a meeting with Allah. One of the three in the room was still alive but just barely. They could not leave someone to talk, so Tracker dispatched him with a two-shot burst to the forehead.

Fathia, scared to death, threw herself into Natty's arms and sobbed. Through sign language and broken English, he had learned during the afternoon that she was born in the oil-rich Sirtica region, where Muammar al-Qaddafi himself was from. Tracker knew Qaddafi's family still lived in Sirte, so he decided he'd take Fathia with them and leave her anywhere but Sirte, since it was heavy with troop concentrations. At this point, he planned to flee Libya by somehow sneaking and fighting his way hundreds of miles eastward to Egypt, by way of the roads that stretched along the Mediterranean. This was the most populated area, and it would be the least expected escape route.

Tracker motioned for Fathia to gather what she could carry while Rabbit returned the MAC-11 to Natty and took a folding-stock AK-47, ammo belt, and several 30-round banana clips from a dead Libyan. The three started to run out the door, but a fusillade of automatic weapons' fire sent Natty flying backward into his companions. Rabbit crawled forward and slammed the heavy door shut with the ball of his foot.

The sounds of thudding boots and shouted commands filled the room through the open window. A soldier's head appeared in the window and Tracker blew it apart with a short burst from his right-hand MAC-11.

Natty was in a real fix now and he knew it. He, Fathia, and Rabbit would have to get away shortly or the whole Libyan army would surround them. He had to come up with a master plan—and quick.

Thunk!

The grenade had flown through the window and landed on the floor. Tracker dived and threw it as soon as his hand touched it. The device exploded just outside the window, and Natty heard a man scream.

He and Rabbit, without a word spoken between them, grabbed a blanket and hung it over the window. It was then that Natty noticed Rabbit's wound. He was bleeding from his right arm. Tracker could see just about everything, but his eyesight was similar to a cheap video picture. The fiber optic filaments attached to his optic nerves created a dot matrix pattern. Like video, the dots were stimulated by whatever patterns the glasses focused on. Natty missed some things unless he saw them close up or squeezed the zoom lens feature built into the frame.

Natty pulled out The Ratel's knife and one of Rabbit's AK bullets. He used the knife to pry the bullet out of the shell and poured the gunpowder into Rabbit's wound. He grabbed a match and prepared to light it.

Sweating, Rabbit said, "Wait, Natty, give me something to bite on."

Tracker laughed and replied, "What do you think this is, Rabbit, some cheap adventure movie? Grit your fucking teeth."

Natty lit the gunpowder; it flared brightly with a foul odor. Gritting his teeth, Rabbit moaned loudly, and miles away, Wally Rampart paced back and forth in a room with two DIA intelligence analysts and several image interpreters. Behind him on a large TV screen, a satellite-view videotape of Tracker's earlier escape and pursuit was running.

Tracker looked out the window and saw the sky darkening. He smiled. He looked up and saw that the ceiling of the flat-roofed stone building was made of old weathered wood. While Rabbit fired out the window, Tracker went to the bedroom and shot several bursts through the roof. To save ammo, he used an AK from one of the dead soldiers.

"Oh shit," Rabbit said grimly after Natty returned and the three heard the popping sound of the Soviet-made helicopter approaching.

Natty grinned and said, "Don't worry, Rabbit. That's what we've been waiting for."

"We have?" Rabbit inquired and ducked with Natty

and Fathia as a tremendous crashing sound erupted directly overhead.

The helicopter set down hard on the flimsy roof, sending dust and splinters down on the seemingly hapless trio. Tracker ran to the bedroom and placed a rickety chair under the spot where he'd fired into the ceiling. He holstered both MAC-11's and turned to face the questioning looks of Rabbit and Fathia.

"I have a plan," he said, smiling broadly. "Trust me, Rabbit."

Rabbit responded sarcastically, " 'Trust me'? That's how people working for the government say 'Fuck you,' Natty."

The helicopter crashed into the ceiling again, loosening a board as Rabbit and Fathia ducked and covered their heads. As they cowered, Tracker reverse punched straight into the ceiling area he'd riddled with bullet holes. A circular piece of roof flew upward, and Natty jumped up, grabbed the edge of the hole, and pulled himself through. He leapt and grabbed the skid of the lifting helicopter, chinning himself up until he sat on the steel runner just below the helicopter's door.

He knocked on the door gunner's side door. It opened. A surprised soldier looked out and Natty yanked him from his perch. The man fell five stories, through the roof of the little house, landing dead not ten feet from a surprised Rabbit and Fathia. Tracker next dived underneath the big chopper, pushing off with his feet, and grabbed the skid on the other side. Pulling himself up and balancing on it, he repeated the same procedure with the other door gunner.

In the meantime, the pilot was maneuvering the craft into position for a rocket shot.

Tracker carefully inched sideways along the port side

skid and opened the pilot's door. The startled pilot and co-pilot looked down at him. A quick burst from the MAC-11 caught the co-pilot in the face, killing him instantly. However, the quick-thinking pilot banked the huge flying weapon to the left. Natty grabbed the webbing of the pilot's safety harness and hung there, his feet dangling in the air.

The pilot flew in a circle, smacking at Natty's fingers. Tracker managed to shove the left-hand MAC-11 into its holster. He reached up with that hand and pulled the pilot's quick-release on the safety harness. With a lunge, he yanked himself up and struck the pilot with a *shuto*, a knife-hand strike right on the point of the Adam's apple. The pilot let go of the controls and grabbed at his throat, his windpipe crushed. The chopper temporarily corrected its attitude.

Tracker again jerked his body up and grabbed the pilot's flight suit with one hand and pulled backward, using his weight to augment the strength of his arms. The pilot, eyes wide open in sheer panic, flew out the door and past Tracker to the hot ground below. Natty then climbed into the cabin and grabbed the controls.

By this time, the soldiers below were able to tell that something was amiss, so several started firing at the helicopter. The rest were unsure who had control so they held their fire.

There was one thing Natty Tracker could do, and that was fly aircraft, any kind, rotary or fixed-wing. He had a working familiarity with this Soviet chopper from classes on enemy aircraft and had only to look over the instrument panel to figure out roughly what did what.

Strapping himself in the harness, he banked the craft into a spiral dive toward the Libyan soldiers and started firing the twenty millimeter cannon. With his night-vision capability, he saw bodies falling everywhere. He followed this with several rockets into the military and police vehicles, frightened soldiers scattering in every direction. He banked again and pulled into a controlled hover over Fathia's house, carefully set the craft down on her roof, and jumped out.

Rabbit looked at the hole in the bedroom ceiling and saw Natty's smiling face appear in the powerful down-draft. He grinned, and at Natty's hand signal, moved Fathia over to the hole and helped pass her into Tracker's waiting arms. Tracker pulled her up and pointed at the door gunner's door. She climbed in and closed it behind her. Simultaneously, Rabbit pulled himself through the hole, crawled under the chopper, and climbed in the co-pilot's door after yanking the bloody corpse out.

As soon as he scrambled into the pilot's seat and closed the door, Tracker revved the engine and lifted off. One brave Libyan soldier had been boosted up by his platoon sergeant to Fathia's roof. As Tracker had done before, the soldier grabbed a skid and clung on, trying to pull himself up.

Natty looked over at Rabbit and said, "Check the skids."

Rabbit held his door open, leaned out, and looked below the chopper. The clinging soldier saw Rabbit and his eyes opened in fear. Rabbit closed his door and smiled at Natty and pointed.

"Got a hitchhiker on the starboard skid," he said.

Tracker grinned and swooped down at the city passing below. He saw a large building that looked fairly modern and raced toward it. They couldn't hear the man's screams or his body slam into the edge of the building's roof as Natty passed over it, expertly maneuvering the chopper's skids within a foot of the rooftop, but both smiled since they knew the result of the dangerous maneuver.

Wally Rampart, watching the helicopter attack and firefight from powerful satellite cameras, again assumed Natty'd been killed. He noticed, however, that the Libyan assault helicopter had headed due north of Tripoli and was heading directly out over the Mediterranean at top speed.

An image interpreter pointed at another monitor and said, "Look, sir."

Wally looked at the satellite view of Wheelus Field which was formerly the largest US Air Force base in the world outside the United States. It was located near Tripoli, and after the US spent two hundred million dollars on it in the fifties and sixties, it was now the proud possession of the Libyan air force. General Rampart watched as two Soviet MIG-23B Flogger jets zipped off the end of the runway and immediately headed toward the fleeing helicopter.

Wally picked up a telephone.

"What's the plan?" Rabbit asked. "Uh-oh," he amended as he looked at two new blips on the radar screen.

"What's up?" Tracker asked.

"We got two bogies on our tail closing fast, partner."

"No sweat," Natty replied. "First, let's go down on the deck."

He put the helicopter into a nearly vertical dive and was soon low-leveling along the surface of the Mediterranean. The helicopter's skids were washed by spray from breaking waves.

Within several minutes the Soviet MIG-23B Flogger jets were close enough to fire at Tracker. He and Rabbit watched the HUD, the heads-up display. A buzzer and flashing light went off.

"They got radar lock-on!" Rabbit shouted, his adrenaline pumping.

He looked back and saw the missile as it was fired at them. It streaked forward and down, and Natty made a series of tight turns. The heat-seeking missile, fired at a downward angle, could not level off fast enough and exploded as its nose struck the surface of the sea at incredible speed. Two more missiles met the same fate.

One of the MIGs came down to near water level and streaked along, opening fire at the helicopter with its machine guns. Tracker pulled into a steep-angle climb, and nearly rolling backward, banked to the right and dived back down. Thus he looped under his previous path and came up just inches from the water, and the MIG-23B flashed by in front of him. He opened up with the twenty millimeter cannons, and the jet streaked into the path of the explosive rounds. It flamed and crashed into the surface of the water. Two minutes later, there was no trace of the downed aircraft except a very small oil slick.

Tracker smiled at Rabbit and asked, "Do you know what the Libyan air force calls the Mediterranean?"

Rabbit grinned, "What?"

"A hangar," Natty replied.

Both laughed.

Then Tracker said gravely, "We've got one other big problem, buddy. The other bogey is a Sierra Hotel (shit hot) pilot. He may lay back and nail us with a Fox-One. We got lucky and nailed his buddy with the Golden BB, but this guy's smarter.'' Both Natty and Rabbit knew they were extremely vulnerable to a Fox-One, a long-range missile attack.

"You'll get us out of it, Natty," Rabbit said confidentially. "You always do."

Tracker said, "Yeah, well, we're in a Sunbeam Mixmaster, pal, and that Libyan is flying at the speed of heat."

"Lock-on!" Rabbit yelled as the buzzer sounded and the light flashed.

"What I wouldn't give for one Lima right now," Tracker said, referring to an AIM-9L Sidewinder missile.

Something flashed past far out over the water, and there was an explosion and a bright flash to their rear. The blip from the MIG-23 Flogger disappeared, but two more appeared to their front.

Tracker grinned and said, "Those are friendlies."

Seconds later, two US Navy F-14 Tomcats streaked past Tracker and dipped their wings from side to side. They both made wide turns and swept back toward Natty as he rocked the chopper from side to side to signal recognition.

The jets slowed to their lowest safe cruising speed and caught up with him and passed by. The Fighter-gators, or Weapons System Operators, in the back seat of both jets held up their fingers indicating a radio frequency. Rabbit turned the dial and found them on the radio. He thanked them and then relayed a message from Natty that he would follow them as far as possible and then auto-rotate into the sea when the chopper ran out of fuel. They radioed ahead to their aircraft carrier, and two rescue helicopters were dispatched.

The President of the United States had been playing tennis with his athletic sons when the call came from Wally Rampart. Sweating, the Chief Executive talked to Wally while he toweled off. He grinned and then laughed.

A Presidential aide knocked and entered the small office near the White House tennis court. He walked over quickly and the President looked up.

"Excuse me, General," the Commander in Chief said into the phone and then looked at the aide.

The aide said nervously, "Mr. President, Muammar Qaddafi's on the telephone with an interpreter and is very angry. He's yelling about us attacking his country and killing innocent people and demands to speak directly to you. What should I tell him, sir?"

The President told Wally that he had to hang up, then he thought for a minute.

He smiled at the aide and said, "Give Qaddafi a message for me."

"Yes, sir?"

The President said, "Tell him I said to go fuck himself."

The President walked out the door, tennis racket in hand, and headed for the tennis court.

Soaking wet, Tracker was hauled into the Navy chopper by electronic winch and joined Rabbit and a very shaky Fathia. Tracker held her in his arms and she started sobbing.

The following day found Fathia in a new apartment in Rome, a city that hosts a large Libyan contingent.

During his debriefing by Wally and a team of intelligence specialists, Natty presented an elaborate scenario about how he had ruined Fathia's life by exposing her as his accomplice. He told them that because she'd aided him and consequently saved the life of the President of the United States, she could never return home and would never see her family again.

What Natty didn't tell them was that her father was a poor goat herder in Sirtica and had traded her for some livestock when she was only thirteen. She had involuntarily become the wife of a Libyan army lieutenant.

Due to Natty's powers of persuasion, Fathia was rewarded with a very comfortable nest egg.

Tracker returned to the United States to undergo a checkup at Walter Reed Army Hospital along with Rabbit. Rabbit was found to be suffering from dehydration, fatigue, and amoebic dysentery. Tracker had to be treated for his amputation and was put on antibiotics to fight possible infection, which miraculously had not yet set in.

Most importantly, because Tracker got word out in time, the President's visit to Israel was cancelled. After a debriefing with Mossad, the crack Israeli intelligence agency, Tracker was sure that the assassination plot would soon be uncovered.

The next day he chuckled as he listened to Tom Brokaw report the accidental death of several Israeli soldiers near Tel Aviv. The soldiers apparently were riding in an Army vehicle on a dirt road outside the city when a huge storm sewer unexpectedly caved in and the men and truck were, in effect, swallowed by the earth. Tracker found the story amusing since Israel is an arid country with little need for large storm sewers, especially in a rural area.

Natty was released from the hospital and delivered to the Oval Office in Marine Corps One, the Presidential helicopter. He had a lengthy meeting with the President, the Secretaries of State and Defense, and Wally Rampart.

Tracker was pledged just about anything within reason, so he requested a sterilized, brand new F-15E Eagle. Unlike the F-15Cs Natty and Rabbit had flown, the new model had more power and more sophisticated avionics equipment. It had two Pratt and Whitney F100-220 engines capable of firing it through space at pressures of nine G-forces. The new Honeywell inertial navigation system was ten times more reliable than its forerunners in the F-15C and F-15D. The Hughes APG-70 radar could actually "see" the ground ahead for eighty miles, and the jet was equipped with two pods underneath that were part of the Martin-Marietta Lantern System. The right-hand pod had a navigation lens that contained the FLIR, Forward Looking Infrared. This part of the Lantern System produced a daylight-quality video image on the heads-up display and had served as a partial model for Natty's OPTIC System. Being "sterilized" as Tracker requested, the jet would have no part that had any stamp, sign, or symbol indicating it had been manufactured in the United States.

The President told the Secretary of Defense to see that the jet was delivered to Tracker in Colorado within the month.

Natty was also given a cash payment of one million dollars from Wally's secret fund. He anonymously donated half of it to AIDS research and the other half to the Muscular Dystrophy Association.

The most important result of his exploits, however, was that Tracker had endeared himself to the United States intelligence community.

He returned to Colorado Springs a satisfied man and began work to upgrade his OPTIC System.

Now, a curved dagger was strapped in a sheath on his right calf. It reminded Tracker that while he could be justifiably proud of his accomplishments, there was still unfinished business that he'd soon have to confront.

13.

Payback Time

THE RATEL SCREAMED and sat up in bed. He was drenched in sweat and was shaking. In the nightmare, Sergeant Rock walked forward, cigar clamped between his teeth in a big grin, and he was holding something in his fingers. He came closer and closer. The object was bloody.

The Ratel looked at his left hand and his ring finger was missing. He looked at Sergeant Rock and his own bloody finger had replaced the cigar in the laughing soldier's mouth.

It was nine hours earlier but exactly the same time half a world away, and Natty Tracker had won the first set of tennis with Dr. Fancy Bird. They met at the net in his tennis court and kissed. A red-tailed hawk circled lazily in the blue sky.

"Have you had enough, Doctor?" Tracker asked.

With a naughty look in her eyes, Fancy said, "No, I haven't. Why don't we go inside?"

Natty grinned impishly, "Should I answer you straight or do you want me to beat around the bush?"

"You know what they say," she said with a flirtatious look. "A Bird in the hand is worth two in the bush."

He grabbed her hand and they walked to the pool area. She fixed him a blackjack on the rocks and made herself a strawberry daiquiri at Natty's poolside bar. The two lay down together in an overstuffed chaise.

Rubbing his cold glass against her sweaty forehead, Tracker said, "Man, is it ever hot today."

She nodded in agreement.

Tracker grinned and picked her up, kicking, laughing, and screaming and dived into the pool. They came to the surface, both laughing, and kissed. Simultaneously, they started removing each other's tennis outfits. Natty dived down and retrieved her glass, which had fallen to the blue-green bottom of the pool. He resurfaced and set it on the pool's edge. Fancy's long auburn hair hung halfway down her tanned back, and Natty took it in his hands and ran them gently through it as his lips closed over hers.

He then kissed her below the breasts and went underwater.

Throwing her beautiful head back and holding the pool's edge, Fancy moaned and groaned.

Two blocks away, three men in Roto-Rooter uniforms sat in a phony maintenance truck. They listened to Fancy's voice and grinned at each other.

She was saying, "Oh, Natty, are you going to come up for air? Oh, you did come up."

Yuri heard a vehicle pull up behind their truck and said, "Ack, nyet."

He stepped out the back door and was greeted by a young pimple-faced Domino's Pizza delivery man.

Yuri said with a thick accent, "Yah, I know. Mister Tracker buy pizza for us."

The young man said, "Yes, sir. Mr. Tracker said that this is a good time for you and your men to take a lunch break, because he said that's what he's going to do."

Yuri laughed as the pizza man got in his Pinto and drove away. He opened the door of the panel truck and heard the sounds of Fancy moaning in ecstasy.

He said in Russian, "Turn everything off and let's eat lunch. Come on, it's pizza again."

That evening, dressed in formal evening attire, Tracker took Fancy down Highway 115 to Florence, Colorado, for dinner at a small, obscure but excellent restaurant named Morelli's Ristorante Italiano. They returned to Colorado Springs and danced in the grand ballroom at the Broadmoor Hotel near Natty's palatial home. They then returned to the house for a nightcap in front of a crackling fire in Tracker's oak-paneled library. This was one of those rare occasions that Natty broke his one-drink-per-day rule.

"I won't be seeing you for a few months," the auburn-haired beauty said.

"Why's that?" Natty asked.

"I'm going on an agency mission to Beirut."

"Beirut . . ." Natty said. "That place is hot, so you be careful. I'm leaving shortly, too, and I'll be in the same part of the world. Maybe we can spend a few days in Rome or Venice after our missions."

"You're going back after The Ratel, aren't you?" Fancy asked.

Natty smiled and held up the stump of his ring finger.

"Are you going to kill him?" she asked.

"Yes," he said seriously.

"Good."

"Good?" he said, surprised.

"Yes—what do you think I am, some wimpy little woman who screams when I see a mouse? I ate mice several times when I ran out of food in the jungle in South America. The world'll be much better off without that scumbag, and you're the man who can do it—maybe the *only* man who can do it."

"I have somebody else to take care of first," Tracker said thoughtfully.

"Who?"

"One of your ex-coworkers, Dr. Edmund Tetrau."

"Oh, yeah, I guess he's almost as responsible for the loss of your finger. Are you going to kill him, too?" she asked.

"No, I can't justify that to myself," Tracker answered. "He lives here in America, not in an enemy country. I can't justify killing people just because they make me mad, but I do need to teach him a lesson."

Fancy said, "You haven't heard about him, then?"

"Heard what?"

"After he left the agency, he immediately joined the Medellin drug cartel in Colombia."

Tracker was shocked. "You're kidding. That changes things. If he joined the drug lords, then he's fair game as far as I'm concerned. Are you sure he didn't just get a job with DIA or DEA or somebody and go under deep cover?"

"Positive," she replied. "We checked it out thoroughly. Besides, can you picture that weasel working undercover on any operation?"

"Point well made. What's he doing for them?"

"None of the established drug wholesalers will have anything to do with him. He pisses off most everybody he comes in contact with. But he knew about a lot of Colombian dealers from our intel files on the cartel, so he's been lining them up with new dealers around the US. If they make a deal, he gets a percentage."

"Can you get me the file on him?"

"Are you kidding, honey? With the reputation you've got in Washington, our people would probably give you the moon for going after that traitor. . . . While we're on the subject, what about the *National Tattler*?" she asked.

"I'm afraid that's something I'll just have to live with. I believe in our Constitution and First Amendment rights, even when they're abused."

One week later, Dr. Edmund Tetrau, driving a rented Cadillac from the Cleveland Airport, pulled into the parking lot of a small restaurant on Tallmadge Avenue in the North Hill section of Akron, Ohio. He got out of the black luxury car, smelled his red rose boutonniere, straightened the lapels on his thousand-dollar blue silk suit, and walked into the restaurant. He sat down with a short stocky man of Italian heritage whom he knew only as Tony. Tony was stocky, slightly bow-legged, and had a small half-moon scar on his chin. He was drinking a rosé wine and motioned for another bottle.

Tetrau loved his new profession since he was treated with respect for the first time in his life. He didn't realize it was because he was doing business with the lowest sleazeballs in the world, and he fit in with them perfectly.

A salt and pepper-bearded Greek Orthodox priest sat in the far corner with a half-eaten plate of spaghetti and a bottle of cheap red wine. Putting his napkin to his mouth, he coughed loudly several times, took a drink of water, and stood. Setting a modest tip on the table, he paid his bill and walked out of the restaurant.

Outside, the priest walked across the busy street and looked around, then got into a red Ferrari Testarossa. He looked around again and removed his beard.

Behind the tinted windows of the car, Tracker scratched his face where the fake beard had been. He reached in his pocket and pulled out the napkin he'd coughed into. Unfolding it, he removed an ultra-thin foot-long blow gun and placed it in a hidden compartment under the dash. He turned on his Blaupunkt stereo CD system, pulled out the cigarette lighter, and plugged in an electronic device with a tiny antenna at the end of it. A wire ran down from it that Tracker plugged into the back of the stereo system. He pushed a button and was rewarded with the clear sounds of Tetrau and Tony deep in conversation in the restaurant.

Above Tony and Edmund's table, a tiny blowgun dart was stuck into the overhead beam. Attached to it was a micro-miniature microphone that picked up and transmitted the sounds from below.

Natty listened with a smile as he heard Tony say, "Now this is my town, man. You don't pay for nothin'. Tell me where you're stayin', Doc. My organization'll take care of the tab, *capish*?"

Edmund was pleased and it showed in his voice. "They referred to it as the intown Holiday Inn on Main Street, as opposed to the downtown Holiday Inn."

Tony laughed, "Yeah, that's true. The downtown Holiday Inn's a coupla miles away. I dunno why they don't give 'em some kinda different fuckin' names, man. It's a fuckin' kick, you know what I mean?"

Tetrau nodded.

Tony continued, "Well, anyhow, you charge anything you want to your room, Doc—broads, booze, whatevah—you want some fuckin' blow to take with you?"

"Sure," Edmund replied, obviously pleased, "thank you, Tony."

"No fuckin' sweat, Doc," Tony said. "You come to Akron, you get treated with class, man."

Tracker laughed to himself at Tony's statement. He started the car and pulled away from the curb.

"Yeah, Tony," Tracker said sarcastically, "you've got tons of class, just like all the other punk drug dealers."

Three hours later, Edmund lay on his hotel bed dressed in black fishnet nylons, black garter belt, and a black leather bra. He gripped his erect penis firmly and pumped it up and down furiously while an acne-faced hooker paced back and forth next to him in soiled lingerie. She half-heartedly kept telling him how she wanted him to beat her. He whimpered when he ejaculated, then he got up, paid her, and cleaned up in the bathroom. The hooker slipped her dress on and left without a word.

In the hotel hallway, she noticed a tall man, his back to her, opening his door. She wondered if she should approach him but decided against it and headed for the elevator. As soon as she entered the elevator, the man walked down the hallway and looked at the number on Edmund's door. The tall man was Nathaniel Hawthorne Tracker.

The morning sun had risen over nearby Quaker Square when the hotel operator rang Edmund's room.

He picked up the receiver and heard a voice tell him that it was eight o'clock. He thanked her and hung up. Tetrau had fallen asleep with the television on, and he looked at the screen now and saw the smiling face of Jane Pauley.

Listening to the morning news on the "Today" show, he got out of bed and walked into the bathroom.

He yawned as he stood in front of the toilet and relieved his bladder. He retrieved his dentures from the jar in which they had been soaking all night, and he placed them in his mouth and bit down on them to push them into a suction-locked position on his gums. Then he went to the sink and turned on the hot water to shave. He looked up to lather his face and screamed in absolute horror. Looking back at him from the mirror was his tired face with a bright red line of lipstick across its throat and the letters R.I.P. printed on the forehead.

His legs gave way under him, and he fell onto the toilet seat. Whimpering again, he jumped up and ran to the door to check the lock and dead bolt. It was secure, so he ran to the window. It was open and Doctor Tetrau looked out and down seven stories. An envelope had been taped directly below his window with duct tape. He again looked and tried to figure out how anybody could have possibly climbed up the building, and he couldn't fathom it. He twisted his head and looked up and saw a lip hanging out above, so he couldn't see how anyone could have rappelled or climbed down to his window. He peeled the envelope off the side of the building and, face pale, sat down on the bed and slowly opened it.

Dear Doctor Tetrau:

You stabbed me in the back. You stabbed your country in the back. Now you're stabbing the backs of countless children and adults. I can get you any time I want, anywhere, and I will . . . soon. I could have poisoned your food last night when you ate with Tony and he offered you booze, broads, and blow. You won't know when it's going to happen or where, and you can't prevent it, but it's going to happen.

Till death do us part,

Trckr

Edmund was visibly shaken and started crying. He threw himself across his bed, racking sobs convulsing his body.

He checked out of the hotel an hour later and got on a plane at the Akron/Canton airport after dropping off his rental car. He was headed to Medellin, Columbia, via connecting flights at Pittsburgh and Miami.

While he was boarding the plane in Pittsburgh, the maintenance man was summoned to Edmund's hotel room in Akron. He had to replace the dead bolt in the door since it had been sawed off cleanly at the door's edge, so if the lever was turned, the door seemed to be locked from the inside. The man couldn't figure it out; it had to have been done from inside the room.

Tracker stood in the Drug Enforcement Agency headquarters in Washington and shook hands with the DEA director, as did Wally Rampart.

"Tracker, I can't tell you how much we appreciate your help," the director said once they were seated.

"My pleasure. Where is he now?" Tracker asked.

The director said, "Our direction-finding aircraft indicate he's on a commercial jet headed south. Probably Miami and then I guess South America. Your plan obviously worked or he would have thrown away the dentures you switched."

Wally clapped Tracker on the back and said, "Good job, Tracker. What do you suppose Edmund Tetrau would say if he knew his teeth are going to tell the DEA the locations and hideouts of major drug buyers and sellers all over the US, South, and Central America?"

Smiling, Natty held his upper and lower lips over his teeth and said, "Hoewy tshit!"

"How long will his dentures keep transmitting for us?" the director asked after a hearty chuckle.

"The battery's good for a year to a year and a half," Natty replied.

"What about your promise to kill him?" Wally asked.

Tracker laughed and said, "Oh, I lied. Considering the people he's dealing with and his incompetence, he'll be dead in less than a year. I just wanted him to die a thousand smaller deaths first. Besides that, the microchip transmitter in his dentures is going to give the DEA a lot of good intelligence until then."

"That's for sure," the director said enthusiastically. "And I'm sending the President a classified letter telling him how much you helped us and how we appreciate it. You let me know if there's ever anything we can do for you."

"Thanks," Natty replied. "Maybe I will sometime."

"Hey, by the way," the director went on, "I heard you lost your finger in Libya. Is that true? They look like they're all there."

Natty held up his left hand, and it looked perfectly normal until he grabbed the end of the ring finger and unscrewed it by twisting the fingernail. The outershell slid off and revealed what appeared to be a fiberglass or nylon core.

Amazed, the DEA chief said, "Prosthetics! Boy, have they changed."

"You got that right," Natty said dryly, and he and Wally exited with a wave.

Outside the building, the two men entered a black limousine and Wally asked Natty, "What do you have in that cylinder in your fake finger?"

Natty smiled and said, "A surprise. Let me test it first, and then I'll let you know what it is and how it works."

"Okay, if you say so. You heading back to Colorado?" Wally asked.

"For a little while."

"Then where?"

"Don't know."

Wally, obviously getting irritated, said, "Tracker, you've been trying to hide something from me, and I think I know what it is. Now tell me—where are you going?"

Tracker stared at Wally through his dark glasses. He was looking at the outlines of the general's head, hairline, eyes, nose, and mouth, but Wally wanted to squirm, thinking Natty was staring into his mind through the amazing OPTIC System.

Tracker spoke calmly, "Rule one, General, and learn it well: I'm an independent contractor and not one of your soldiers, nor am I one of your government employees. Where I go on my own time is none of your fucking business.''

"Pull over," the undersecretary growled at the limo driver.

The black auto pulled over to the curb, and the general jumped out, snapping at Natty, "Wait here."

He pulled out a cigar and lit it, clamping down with his teeth. Hands folded behind his back, he stormed down the sidewalk, eyebrows furled in anger.

Natty grinned as he watched him, leaned forward, and tapped the shoulder of the driver/secret service agent who was inching forward, following the angry old soldier.

Tracker said, "Look at him with that stogey in his mouth, stalking along with his hands behind his back. Doesn't he look like Winston Churchill?"

The agent laughed and replied, "You're right, he does. Joe Piscopo couldn't do a better impression."

After fifteen minutes, Wally Rampart climbed back in the limousine. He looked straight ahead and gritted his teeth. Natty could feel icicles in the air.

Teeth still clenched tightly and looking straight ahead, he finally spoke. "You're right. I stepped on my dick—with track shoes. I apologize."

He reached his hand to Tracker and shook hands with him.

Natty, smiling broadly, said cheerfully, "I'm going after The Ratel."

Wally sighed. "I'm against it, Tracker."

"I know; I respect that."

"Something you got to do?" Wally asked, still tight-lipped.

"Yes."

The old warrior relaxed, faced Natty, and said, "If it's what you got to do, let me know what you need. I'll give you anything you need in the way of support."

"Thanks, General. Appreciate it," Tracker said.

"What do you need, son?" the undersecretary asked.

Natty looked at him squarely and said, "Prayers."

14.

Back into the Jaws of Death

THERE IS A large flat-topped-plateau, or hamada, due south of Tripoli named Hamada el-Homra. Covered with coarse dark stones for the most part, it's a deserted area and was where Tracker had decided to make his infiltration. He had developed some new electronic devices and a special vehicle for this trip, but he hadn't had time to test them thoroughly.

He took off from Lisbon, Portugal, went straight across the Strait of Gibraltar and took a 1,200 mile zigzagging course that brought him in across the Atlas Mountains in Morocco almost due south of Tangiers. He crossed into Algeria over the majestic Sahara desert west of Bechar. Streaking along the deck the whole time, Natty eluded radar detection.

He pushed his powerful twin-thruster F-15E Eagle, specially equipped for this mission, along the western edge of the Great Western Erg and the Tademait Hamada. He then turned due east and passed along the steep walls of the southern edge of the Tademait Hamada and north of the city of Ain Salah. He low-leveled northeast over the Tinrhert Hamada, crossed the border into Libya and turned north toward Tripoli. He zoomed across the Hamada el-Homra without seeing a soul.

He chose to land and hide his jet in a deserted area roughly at the apex of the cities of Mizda, Nalut, and Sinawan. When he found a long flat area, Tracker dropped his landing gear, specially fitted wheels with balloon-type dune buggy tires. The landing was a bit rougher than most, but the jet came safely to a halt.

The Libyan air force had ten French Mirage III jet reconnaisance fighters, along with two dozen Soviet Migs, and 124 other Mirage jets which were all fighter-bombers, 12 Soviet Tupolev-22 Blinder bombers, eight French Magister jets, and most importantly, 200 Italian-made SF-260W Warrior jets configured specially for counterinsurgency operations. This was just part of the Libyan air force, so Natty knew he had to hide his jet well.

He hit two release levers and the pods below the ends of both wings dropped to the ground with a thud. He climbed down and chocked the wheels and then walked to the left pod and opened the hatch on its side. He extracted a nylon camouflage tarpaulin that had the exact colorings and markings of the rocky ground he was on, and the other side was the exact color of the seas of sand in the Sahara. He then went to the right-hand pod, pulled four steel pins, and the pod unfolded into a flat metal rectangle. A large vinyl ring fell around it. Natty unscrewed what looked like a garden faucet handle, pulled another pin in a steel cylinder head, and there was a loud hissing sound as the vinyl ring started filling with air.

Within minutes the steel frame rested within the protective confines of the vinyl ring that now lifted it about three feet off of the ground.

In the center of the little vehicle was a long crooked steering handle and two pedals. There was also a seat above a square box that housed the engine. A big steel post rose up from the compartment behind the driver's seat. Tracker went to the left pod and pulled out three small propeller blades and went back to the little craft and turned it over on its side. Using a tool kit also retrieved from the pod, he attached the three blades underneath the vinyl ring, making it look like a giant power lawn mower. He connected two hoses underneath which came from the engine compartment.

Tracker was anxious to see how his little craft was going to run. He had designed it, but it had actually been built by several government defense contractors. He went back and climbed to the canopy of the jet. He reached inside and set three large rotor blades and a six-foot section of tubing on the wing. He jumped down and carried them one by one to the small craft.

He first attached an extension onto the thick steel post behind the driver's seat and attached the two longest rotor blades to it. It now became obvious that this craft was some kind of helicopter. He unfolded the tubing and fitted it to the back, forming a tiny tail section for the helicopter. He attached a machine chain to a small gearbox in the tail section and hooked up several cables. He next attached the smaller tail rotor blade to it.

Tracker screwed a box of 7.62 millimeter machine gun ammunition to the front of the platform followed by an M-60 machine gun. He loaded the gun and test fired a quick burst of six. He then connected an electronic device to the gun's trigger mechanism, which had wires running to a fighter pilot's helmet. Natty sat in the seat, put on the helmet, and twisted his head from right to left. The machine gun moved with his head, and he put what looked like a computer mouse mounted in front of the helmet between his teeth. When he bit down, the M-60 fired another burst of six rounds.

Natty also installed a small, four-barrel weapon that had been made from four M-79 grenade launchers. He pushed a lever to the side and the barrels broke down. He loaded four high explosive grenades into the chambers and closed it. He attached a wire to a plug on the steering tiller. He checked the top of the tiller and made sure the switch by the button read SAFE. He put on the leather harness and the twin shoulder holsters with the MAC-11s and attached a pack to the back of the platform.

He climbed to the jet canopy again, reached inside the cockpit, removed a safety release pin, and pushed a button that read BTFOOAI. Wally had loved this little button, as the letters stood for Blow The Fuck Out Of Any Intruders. It was an arming device designed to make the jet explosively self-destruct if anyone tried to climb inside, handle the controls, move it, or even bump it too hard.

Natty then covered the jet with the huge camouflage tarp. He placed rocks around all of the edges to hold it in place despite the fierce desert winds. He placed a plastic five gallon can of fuel into a box built for it on the platform and climbed into the seat, strapped himself in, and crossed his fingers.

He pushed down on a plunger and released it, and the small engine started up with a high-pitched whine. There was a big lever next to the pilot's seat which was now on neutral. Straight forward it read ROTORS, and straight back, HOVER. Natty pulled the lever straight back and a sound like a big vacuum cleaner competed with the engine noise. The vinyl sides came off the ground six inches as the hovercraft rose on a cushion of air.

Natty tried the throttle and controls, and everything checked out perfectly. He pushed the handle forward to neutral, let the craft settle down to the ground, and then he pushed the handle forward to the helicopter mode. The rotor blades started whirring, and he lifted off the rocky surface to hover twenty feet off of the ground. Natty again checked the controls and all were functional. He set down and shut the craft down.

The craft had been christened the Hovercopter by Natty and the aeronautical engineers who had worked with him on it. They were anxious to see how it was going to work on this mission, and so was the Department of Defense, since weapons analysts were excited about testing the Hovercopter for use by the US Army and Marine Corps.

Tracker pulled a metal box out of his pack, set it down, and unfolded it. Several small square mirrors unfolded and faced the hot desert sun. It was a solar-powered stove. He boiled water and had a meal of dehydrated spaghetti, meat balls, and hot coffee. He then took two salt tablets, forced himself to drink a quart of water, packed everything up, and climbed into the pilot's seat. He cranked up the Hovercopter and took off toward the capitol of Libya, 130 miles to the northeast.

The flight was uneventful until he was a short distance outside Yefren in the area called the Gebel Nefusah. As he cruised aloft, the revised Tracker device on his left wrist started flashing. Natty set down and transferred to hover mode. The device indicated multiple targets two kilometers to the front. He went forward at full speed and had them in sight within a minute. They saw him, and he stopped and set down on fine, tan-colored sand, clouds of it blowing up around the Hovercopter.

Natty looked at the group of men and squeezed the frame on his glasses. He zoomed in to look at a Soviet T-72 battle tank and two Soviet BMP-76 armored personnel carriers. The column was led by a British Ferret armored car.

Tracker figured they were out on maneuvers or convoying somewhere to go on maneuvers. In either event, he knew they had to have weapons with live ammo or they wouldn't be out in such an isolated area. Natty also knew that they had radios, and that meant they had to be silenced. The question was: how? Natty had a grenade launcher, a light machine gun, and two machine pistols. Facing a Soviet BMP-76 tank, he might as well have had a slingshot and a BB gun.

The column was several hundred yards away and headed straight for him. He saw someone look out of the armored car with a pair of binoculars, so he smiled broadly and waved. The man in the car smiled and waved back.

Tracker reached into his pack and pulled out the bottle of alcohol he carried to disinfect wounds. He drained the alcohol, poured gasoline into the bottle from the gas can, and then shoved a sock into the bottle's neck. He climbed back into the Hovercopter, put it in flight mode, and took off after lighting his Molotov cocktail. He flew directly at the soldiers who were obviously puzzled. He hoped they hadn't radioed their headquarters yet.

Still waving and smiling, he pulled into a hover twenty feet above the tank. Now, men were waving at Natty from each of the vehicles.

He smiled, produced his expedient bomb and dropped it directly on the air louvers above the tank's engine. There was a blast of fire and smoke as the flaming liquid made its way into the engine compartment.

Natty bit the trigger mechanism and gunned down the exposed soldiers before they realized what was happening. Then he concentrated on one goal: knocking out the radio antennae on each vehicle. He accomplished this by firing rifle grenades at almost pointblank range.

Bullets tore at the small craft from both APCs. He turned sharply, pulled out his left-hand MAC-11, and swept in firing that and the M-60, wiping out both machine gunners. He felt several bullets brush past his cheek, but miraculously, his craft was essentially untouched.

He then reloaded the M-79 grenade launchers and fired it to finally disable each vehicle. A bullet came through the platform, and Natty screamed in pain as it tore through his right thigh. That made him angry.

Men started piling out of the crippled vehicles and fired up at him, taking refuge behind the steel monsters. Tracker dived straight at the gunfire, biting down with his teeth and firing the MAC-11s left and right. Then with his right hand, he hit the tiller trigger four times as quickly as he could to launch four grenades. He swept in so close that, as he passed over, a piece of shrapnel from the last grenade flew up and put a razor-sharp cut in Natty's forehead and imbedded itself in the front of his helmet lining.

Tracker's thigh burned and ached, but he put it out of his mind. Even so, he couldn't ignore the blood that was now flowing into his eyes. He headed straight away from the action for a distant sand dune where he set the chopper down. Natty unhooked his safety harness and jumped out with the out-of-range Libyan soldiers taking a sporadic "Hail Mary" shot at him.

He reached back, grabbed the plastic gas can, and placed it next to his seat. He pulled out a T-shirt from his pack, tore it into strips, and wrapped one strip around his thigh and the other around his forehead. He then took off directly at the remaining soldiers. They began firing before they should have, but Natty didn't notice. He grabbed the can of gas and unscrewed the cap. Braving the fire, he plunged straight ahead firing the M-60 with his teeth.

Closing in on the remaining Libyans, Natty made them all duck for cover by firing the M-79s again. He pulled back when he zoomed in over their heads and started lowering the aircraft in a hover, counting on the downblast from the rotors to keep the soldiers' heads down. Luckily, he was correct. Hovering, Natty held the steering tiller between his knees and poured the gas out over the screaming soldiers and vehicles below.

He pulled out of the hover and circled, bullets flying at him from some, while several, sensing what was coming, tried to run. Natty buzzed over them and fired a flare gun, igniting the gas in a giant ball of flame. He had to hold the tiller tightly because of the concussion. This was followed by two secondary explosions when the ammo in one APC and the gas tank of the armored car both exploded. Natty set down and got out of the helicopter.

Holding both MAC-11s, Tracker walked cautiously forward and found that all the Libyan soldiers were dead. Natty stared into the flames and looked at the dead bodies. Anyone who claims to be a warrior and has looked at his enemies fallen before him without

feeling remorse is either a liar or sick. Tracker felt saddened, very much so, but he had a mission to accomplish, so he shoved his negative feelings into the deeper
recesses of his mind.

Tracker took a reading on the Tracker System and
determined he was alone in the desert. He walked to
the Hovercopter, looked down, and saw small dog-like
tracks in the sand. He recognized them as the pawprints
of a Fennec fox, a species found all over the Sahara.
They made Natty realize that the desert was also a place
full of life, not just death.

He hoped that the Libyan people of the great desert
could someday enjoy their country's riches and get out
from under the fanaticism of Muammar al-Qaddafi. He
decided that he would do everything he could to oust
the madman . . . But first, he would deal with The
Ratel.

Tracker lifted off and low-leveled toward his objective. He came down off the hamada and went back into
the hovercraft mode. He also made a mental note that
he'd have to steal some gas somewhere, or he'd never
make it back to his hidden jet. The engine of the Hovercopter was smaller than that of a Volkswagen and got
extraordinary mileage, but he'd still need at least three
gallons for the return trip.

Bypassing all civilization, Tracker made his way to
the high-walled prison by nightfall. He left the craft
about a mile away and marched through the sand after
drinking liberal amounts of water. People have different
theories about drinking water in the desert. Knowing
that perspiration hits the skin and immediately evapo-
rates, Tracker held to the theory that consuming as
much as possible whenever water was available was
best. This not only deterred dehydration but helped

prevent the formation of kidney stones and other maladies that could develop when the body's moisture content fell to dangerously low levels.

Tracker sneaked as close as possible to the prison's southern wall. What he was going to attempt was daring, perhaps foolhardy. He squeezed the frames of his glasses and they zoomed his vision into a close-up. Natty lay there motionless and watched the guards on the south wall and the southern towers until just before daybreak. Then he crept away and returned to his vehicle and left.

Natty hid and camped in a cypress grove in a wadi, a narrow canyon, he found a few miles away. In the wadi was a guelta, a permanent desert water hole. Shielded from some of the desert sun, the guelta was undisturbed except by the animals and birds that came to drink from its life-giving pool. Some vegetation grew around it and provided countless insects for the birds that came.

Natty thought about the life that flourished in the desert as he ate lunch and watched a pair of crag martins playing above. He chuckled as he recalled the Sahara in many feature films he had seen, and in no case had it been depicted properly. In every single movie, the Sahara was shown only as a vast ocean of sand dunes, but in actuality the sand dunes comprise only one-fourth of the desert. The rest is mountains, plateaus, gravel plains, and various rocky formations.

The following night, Natty lay outside the prison looking at the men on the east wall and adjacent towers. Again, he remained all night observing the guards and returned to the wadi just before daybreak.

The third night he repeated the procedure, watching

the north wall, and the fourth night he returned to observe the west wall.

On the fifth night, Natty Tracker didn't come just to watch. He had determined that almost all the guards fell asleep shortly after going on duty. Natty had seen this in some American military units also and found it difficult to believe. It had not been that long since he'd breached the walls of this very prison and had killed many of the compatriots of these guards. Still, these undisciplined, unmotivated soldiers fell asleep without even trying to stay awake. He had noted that the guards on the south wall were the most lax, so that was where he would launch his assault.

He watched until he was certain that all were asleep, and then he ran forward in diving rushes. Natty reached the wall unseen and stopped to catch his breath. He was dressed in the garb of the ninja, the invisible assassins of Japan. In actuality, the ninja hit men of old primarily killed their enemies by poisoning their food, not by hand-to-hand combat as films depict, but Natty felt that the black outfit was most apropos for this part of the mission.

He slipped a pair of glove-like devices and modified boots out of his pack and put them on. The gloves had steel climbing spikes welded into the frames that covered them, and the boots were similar. With them, he would be able to scale the wall by inserting the slightly curved spikes into the cracks between the big stones.

It was a long climb straight up, but Natty was an athlete in very good condition. At the top, he slid over the wall and found himself face-to-face with a sleeping guard. Tracker checked out the prison yard below, and finding it empty, he scaled down the inside of the wall.

Carefully, he made his way through the shadows to

the door from which he and Rabbit had made their mad dash for freedom. It was locked. Undaunted, Natty reached into a side pocket on his pack and removed a small tool kit. He opened its Velcro fastener and pulled out a rake and pick, the two tools used by all good burglars to pick locks. He applied side pressure on the lock with the pick and started moving tumblers out of the way with the rake. Within seconds, the lock gave way, and Natty carefully opened the heavy door and slipped inside.

He looked around carefully. The sound of snoring came from the room which held The Ratel. He sneaked inside quietly and crept over to the bed where the unsuspecting guerrilla slept. Tracker looked closely and saw that this was not the notorious terrorist. He figured that this must be a guard Pedro was using as a decoy. He had probably heard of the attack on the armored unit out in the desert and was taking no chances.

Natty didn't know that The Ratel had started this practice the day after Natty's escape.

Tracker went steathily down the steps and made his way to the room that still had *National Tattler* pages taped to the walls. He went past the interrogation room and down to the sand-floored hallway leading to the cells. He looked into each cell, and in the second one, he saw The Ratel sleeping fitfully. He grinned to himself. It would be easy to enter the cell and kill the man while he lay there or even wake him and then kill him. This was not Natty's plan, however. He had planned this and thought about it for too long.

Tracker went to the next cell and picked the lock. He entered and immediately removed his pack, took out a folding shovel, and started digging. He buried the pack deep in the sandy floor. Natty left the cell and looked in on Pedro as he passed by and saw he was still asleep. He then made his way down the hallway and up the stairs.

As Natty made his way to the big door, he didn't hear the guard snoring, so he froze in place. The tumblers in the lock on the door made a noise, and he quickly flattened against the wall next to the door. The guard walked in the door zipping his pants. Yawning, he turned and locked it, not noticing Tracker six feet away.

The guard went into the room and lay down. Natty waited until the snoring was loud again before he moved. He stole into the darkened room and walked out with the door key. He had kept the rake and pick, sliding them into a pouch in his sleeve, but the key was much easier.

Once in the courtyard, he stayed in the shadow of the doorway and looked at the walls. A guard was pacing back and forth on the south wall. Tracker didn't blink an eyelid.

When the guard turned away, Natty reached down the back of his shirt and pulled out a telescoping blowgun. Extremely accurate, even at long distances, the blowgun could be a very potent weapon if used correctly. Tracker didn't understand why it wasn't used more often in commando-type operations. He pulled a small leather bag out of the cargo pocket on the side of his trouser leg. He opened it and removed a blowgun dart with a small-gauge hypodermic needle sticking from it. Natty removed the cup from the dart and attached it to a hypodermic tube. He inserted the needle into a small bottle of liquid, withdrew several cc's, and replaced the dart cup. After putting the packet back into his pants, Natty loaded the dart into the blowgun. He watched the guard carefully and shot. The dart struck the man in the neck and he fell instantly.

Natty waited a full five minutes to insure no one else had heard and then ran over and scaled the wall. He climbed along the top until he found the dead guard lying in the walkway, picked the man's body up, and dropped it over the side. The man would be missed in the morning, but Tracker assumed that the Libyan army had a high rate of desertion.

He climbed down the outside wall, picked the man up over his shoulder and took off toward the distant Hovercopter. Over the first dune, however, Natty stopped and buried the guard's body. He made it to the Hovercopter and took off for his hideout.

Tracker slept all day, awakened, and prepared a meal. After he packed up, he returned to the prison. Natty threw a grappling hook up with a rope attached and started scaling the south wall. At the top, he saw that all the guards were again asleep. He tossed the rope down the other side, started climbing down, and the guards still slept. Halfway down, Natty paused and coughed loudly. He continued down the wall and dropped to the ground below. Tracker saw several men stirring after his cough, so he knew what was coming. Spotlights hit him from two towers, and machine gun bullets kicked up sand at his feet as he threw his hands up.

Within thirty seconds, Tracker was surrounded by angry Libyan army soldiers. They removed the twin Browning nine-millimeter High Powers from his shoulder holsters. The twin MAC-11s were hidden inside Natty's pack in the floor of the third cell.

The Ratel came out of the main prison complex and a big grin spread across his face. He motioned for sev-

eral guards to seize Natty and take him inside. He led
the way and they followed.

Downstairs in the prison, The Ratel stopped at the
first cell, opened the door, turned, and gave Natty a
knowing look.

He grinned and said, "No."

He closed the door and led them down to the third
cell and opened the door. Natty was troubled because
Pedro had paused at the first cell.

Pedro spoke again as Natty was tossed into the cell
and landed hard on the bunk, "Welcome, Señor
Tracker, I have been expecteeng you."

Tracker could hear The Ratel laughing loudly as he
walked down the hallway. A cold chill ran down Natty's
spine. Within a minute, he heard The Ratel and several
guards heading back toward his cell. Natty sat on the
bunk and looked ahead as the cell door opened. The
Ratel appeared in the doorway holding Tracker's rucksack in his right hand.

"Amigo," The Ratel said gleefully, "I theenk you
maybe have beeg brass balls. You sneaked eento thees
preeson sometime and buried that pack. You just got
caught on purpose, Tracker, 'cause you wanted to make
mee feel good and then spoil my party and keel me."

He continued, "What you deedn't know was that the
sergeant of thee guard got heemself a metal detector
and checks thee sand all over thees preeson all thee
time. He ees always finding coins and theengs. Deed
you know that he was just made the rank of *Mulazim
Awwal* by Colonel Qaddafi heemself? That ees the same
as thee rank of First Lieutenant een your army. You
know why the Colonel promoted heem?"

"Why?" asked Natty.

"Beecause, I tell heem thees pack beelonged to you

and I would catch you, mee amigo. He wants your head very bad, Tracker. I weel geeve eet to heem, but first I weel mail your Presidente more pieces of your body. One piece each day unteel you die. What do you think of that, Tracker?''

Tracker grinned and said, ''I was just wondering—if that dick-brain you're working for is the head of this whole country, then why in the hell does he give himself the title of colonel? Why the hell doesn't he at least call himself a general?''

The Ratel was angry, but he smiled and said, ''You know, amigo, you always theenk you are clever, but now I have another surprise for you, so come weeth me—please?''

Pedro nodded and two guards held AK-47s on Natty while two more bound his hands with cuffs and locked his ankles in shackles. They led him to the interrogation room and hooked his cuffs to the ceiling and his shackles to the floor. The Ratel nodded to the guards, they left the room, and Pedro, grinning like a Cheshire cat, sat behind the table and looked up at Natty.

''You know, Tracker, you have beeen een beesiness for only a short while and already the whole world knows of you—thee eemportant people, that ees. When I slowly keel you, can you imageen what eet weel do for me?''

Natty spit across the room at Pedro, who laughed loudly.

''I theenk maybe theengs are not goeeng as you planned, mee amigo,'' the terrorist said. ''And jus' wait unteel you see my beeg surprise for you. You weel be most upset. You know I have frens I work for all over the Meedeast, Tracker, and guess who some of my frens caught?''

The door opened and Tracker heard a familiar voice scream, "Natty!"

Tracker watched in horror as two guards carried a battered, bruised, and naked Fancy Bird past him. She was shackled to a table hand and foot. Both of her eyes were blackened and both nipples had dark bruises around them.

"Fancy!" Tracker cried. "Don't worry, I'll get you out of here."

The Ratel burst out in laughter and said, "Tracker, you are eemposseeble! You speak of saveeng her. I weel show you how much power you have, amigo. Guard, come heer and point your gun at Tracker's head. Eef she does not do exactly as I say, shoot heem."

A guard walked over, cocked a Swedish K, and put the muzzle against Natty's temple. Fancy's eyes opened in abject fear as The Ratel walked toward her unzipping his pants. He pulled out his now-erect penis and pushed it at her mouth.

Natty lost control and started screaming, "Don't do it, Fancy! Pedro, I'll kill you, you son of a bitch! If you kill me, I'll come back from hell and kill you, you motherfucker!"

The Ratel just grinned over his shoulder and forced her to fellate him. Tears ran down her cheeks, and she screamed as he then placed himself between her legs and raped her, plunging violently over and over until he ejaculated.

All the while, Natty screamed at him until he was hoarse. The Ratel walked back to Natty, smiling evilly as he put his penis back in his pants.

"Nice pussy, amigo, but I guess you already know that, huh? Tomorrow, she weel suck me in front of you, and I weel also cut off one of your ears and mail eet to your Presidente. We weel do the same each day,'' he said sadistically. ''Take them both back to their cells,'' he directed to the guards.

Tracker wasn't speaking any more He just stared at The Ratel, and the look and the silence gave Pedro a shaking chill that ran up and down his spine. There was something about Tracker that made him very uncomfortable.

Fancy was tossed into the first cell, and Natty, still silent, was taken to his cell and thrown in. He immediately lay down on his bunk, closed his eyes, and tensed his entire body. Next, Natty started relaxing all of the muscles in his head and neck. He then relaxed his shoulder muscles, upper arms, and upper back and chest, then lower arms and abdomen, followed by buttocks, hands, and lower back, then thighs, calves, and finally his feet.

He let himself totally relax as he breathed through his nose and programmed himself to awaken in one hour. He was disappointed in himself for screaming until he was hoarse. It may have encouraged The Ratel, and it certainly hadn't helped Fancy. Tracker always fared better in an emergency when he exuded his quiet strength.

He vowed that he would never''lose it'' again in an emergency, no matter what. He wasn't upset that his plans had gone awry and that he hadn't simply sneaked into the prison, killed The Ratel, and left. Had he not allowed himself to be captured, he wouldn't now have a chance to save Fancy, who had been captured in Beirut.

Tracker also wondered how The Ratel knew enough about him to know about his relationship with Fancy. It only took a moment's thought to come up with the answer to that. But that was a matter that he'd deal with later.

He went to sleep.

Fancy lay on the dank cot and wept and shook. Tears streaked down her face as she relived the humiliating, painful, and horrifying experience. She felt dirty. She felt like a mechanic's dirty, greasy shop towel, carelessly thrown on a filthy garage floor and picked up whenever needed again.

That was the second time Ratel had raped her, and it had been in front of the man she loved. The thought hit her. It was her first realization that she was in love with Natty Tracker. A new resolve gripped her: she *would* survive this, and she would castrate The Ratel.

Someday, she would marry and have children. She might even marry Natty Tracker, but first she'd do everything she could to make the world a safer place to bring children into. For now, she made a priority decision: to survive this.

The Ratel went to his room excited. He remembered the screaming of the woman and Tracker both. The terror they felt made his adrenaline flow. He couldn't sleep, so he had a guard bring him one of the Libyan political prisoners from the first floor of the prison. Once in his room, he made the frightened young man strip and bend over. Then he brutally sodomized him, reveling in the man's screams of pain and fear. Then he sent the prisoner away; soon after, he fell asleep feeling happy. •

* * *

The Ratel was fighting wave after wave of armed American soldiers, slashing left and right with the curved dagger he'd retrieved from Natty Tracker. They all screamed in pain as they fell before his blows, and a foul wind blew through his hair. He had killed so many enemy soldiers that the blood was flowing above his knees.

In the distance, he saw Sergeant Rock smiling, cigar clenched between his teeth, walking forward through the charging soldiers. He still stabbed and slashed and cut, Americans falling all about him, but Sergeant Rock just kept coming. He not only smiled but laughed as well, and Pedro was gripped by fear. It turned to panic as Sergeant Rock advanced. Sergeant Rock's face suddenly turned into the visage of Natty Tracker and he laughed heartily. Pedro stabbed him with the bloody dagger, but the knife went in and bounced out of Tracker's body as if it were rubber. Tracker laughed as Pedro stabbed him again and again. Then Tracker held up his hand and pulled off the end of his left ring finger, and poisonous snakes crawled out of the stump of the finger. They flew through the air at Pedro's face and he started screaming.

Yelling, "No! No! No!" Pedro sat up, his body shaking.

Hearing the screams, a guard ran to Pedro's door, and Pedro grabbed Natty's MAC-11 and fired, killing the guard instantly. Pedro got up and realized what had happened. He was breathing heavily and sweat stung his beady eyes.

A revelation hit him in the pit of the stomach; something had been different about Tracker, but he hadn't been able to pinpoint it until now. Tracker had all ten of his fingers. He panicked and ran out the door of his room with both of Natty's MAC-11s. Then he heard a small explosion about as loud as a high caliber rifle shot.

Tracker awoke, stretched his leg and arm muscles, and relieved his bladder, preparing for combat. He unscrewed his finger and removed the nylon core. He shook three plastic balls from it and held them in his other hand while he replaced the cylinder and screwed the prosthetic finger back on.

Natty inserted one of the balls in the keyhole of the cell door and removed the mattress from his cot. He leaned the cot frame against the door so it made contact with the plastic ball and shielded himself with the mattress. He gave the top of the frame a slight push and dropped to the floor, covered by the mattress. The plastic ball exploded and destroyed the lock.

Tracker ran out of the cell and a burst of gunfire from his own MAC-11 greeted him.

Scared but grinning, The Ratel walked forward, brandishing Natty's machine pistols. Instead of ducking, Natty jumped straight up in the air and executed a flying front snap kick that shattered the long light bulb illuminating the hallway. Hearing distant shouts from guards, Natty hit the floor and rolled as bursts kicked up sand around him.

The Ratel had weapons but could not see now, and Natty could. Natty laughed and dived forward, hit the ground in a somersault, and came up running. The Ratel fired blindly in the narrow hallway, and Natty watched closely and dodged the gunfire. He threw the second plastic ball, and it struck Pedro in the right kneecap and exploded, nearly tearing the man's leg off. Tracker ran forward and kicked the two guns from Pedro's hands and picked them up.

Leaving Pedro there, he ran for the steps and raced up them two at a time. An angry mob of guards was starting down the stone stairway when Natty rounded the last turn, He fired at them with both guns, and a wave of them went down under the withering hail of bullets. They backed up as a group, and Natty threw the second plastic ball. It struck one of the lead guards in the face and blew his head off. The rest ran out the door followed closely by Natty. He fired several bursts into the backs of the fleeing soldiers, then locked the door behind them with the keys that hung on a nearby hook.

He ran into The Ratel's room and retrieved his pack, rapidly checked the contents, and grabbed the big ring of keys for all the cells. He ran back down to the cell-block and kicked the curved dagger from the hand of The Ratel as he stepped over him in the darkness. He unlocked Fancy's door.

"Fancy, it's me," he said calmly. "C'mon, time to jump in the Batmobile and head for the Bat-cave."

"Oh, Natty!" she said with a rush of breath, relief flooding her being.

She stumbled out the door and into his arms where she shook and trembled, still naked.

"Do you know where your clothes are?" he asked.

"One of the guards took them."

In the darkness, he handed her both MAC-11s and pointed through the dank passageway to the winding staircase.

"Get up there fast, honey," he commanded, "and fire out the window in the door every time you see anything move."

"Okay," she yelled back, bare feet padding up the steps at a dead run. He heard her firing after a few seconds, and he turned to reenter the darkened hallway. Adrenaline pumping, Tracker picked up The Ratel by the back of the neck and retrieved the curved dagger from the sandy floor. He pulled The Ratel to the stairs and dragged the profusely bleeding terrorist up with him. He dropped Pedro on the floor near the big door. Smiling and flipping the dagger in the air and catching it by the handle, he looked down at the shaking guerrilla leader.

"I made you a promise, Pedro," Natty said.

"Wait!" Fancy screamed. "Natty, come here and watch the door. I made *myself* a promise."

Natty handed her the knife and walked over to the door, quickly firing a burst out the window just to let the guards know they were still there. There were a few answering shots from the wall.

The Ratel was too weak from loss of blood to do anything but shake. He was trying hard to be brave and hardcore to the end, but his resolve was faltering as the naked spy unhooked his pants and pulled them down. He started screaming as she grabbed his testicles in her hand and grinned evilly.

Fancy stared hard into his frightened eyes and said coldly, "This is not just for me, but for every woman you've raped and terrorized, you son of a bitch."

He screamed at the top of his lungs as she cut off his testicles and stuffed them in his shirt pocket. She then cut off his penis and stuck it in the other pocket and calmly walked over to Tracker. The Ratel kept looking down at his bloody crotch and sobbed like a frightened child.

Fancy handed the knife to Natty, took the guns, and looked out the door. Tears ran down her cheeks, and she felt light-headed. Her knees buckled, but she caught herself and forced herself to be calm to do her job.

Natty grabbed a pan of water and tossed it on Pedro's face. Pedro was starting to go into shock, but the water revived him slightly.

Tracker said, "This is for every man, woman, and child you've murdered. For every bomb you've planted. For every terrorist you've trained. For every American you've hurt, you evil bastard."

Tracker lifted the terrorist's left hand and cut off the ring finger which brought renewed and strengthened screaming from The Ratel. His eyes opened wide in absolute horror as Natty tried to pry his mouth open.

The Ratel clamped his teeth together, so Natty inserted the dagger's blade in his mouth and pried the teeth apart. He shoved the bloody finger into Pedro's throat while the man wet himself and voided his bowels.

Pedro, eyes bulging, choked and gasped and tried to cough the finger out, but Natty shoved it back in with the blade of the knife. Finally, Tracker struck The Ratel across the throat with the blade of his hand, breaking the finger lodged in his throat and crushing the demon's windpipe as well. Gurgling sounds came from The Ratel's throat as blood spilled from his mouth, and his eyes rolled back in his head. He died . . . as he'd lived—violently.

Tracker headed for the stairway but stopped before going down. "Fancy," he said, "I'll leave the door propped open so you can see in the hallway. As soon as you hear a loud explosion downstairs, run down and come to my cell, the third one. I'll be there waiting for you."

The soldiers started taking more chances, and Fancy

killed several more. She was getting impatient after five minutes passed, but finally there was a loud explosion. She ran downstairs and into the hallway. It was filled with smoke, and there was a gaping hole in the wall where the barred window had been. Outside, a long string of firecrackers was going off, and shots rang down from the prison walls. She could hear the shouts of Libyan soldiers as she ran into Tracker's cell and into his arms.

Within five minutes, the prison was filled with shouting soldiers. Most stayed by the hole in the wall and pointed at the outside wall closest to the hole. A grappling hook was anchored at the top of the wall and a knotted rope hung down to the prison yard. The front gates opened and vehicles started up and poured out into the desert night. Some made circles out in the desert while others headed for Tripoli. Occasional shots rang out in the desert.

In Natty's cell, the sand moved and then poured off the sand-colored tarpaulin as Natty and Fancy stood up in the hole he'd dug in the soft sand. He hugged her and brushed away a tear with his index finger.

He took the still-nude beauty by the hand and led her carefully up the now-deserted stairway. She had donned the double shoulder holsters with the Browning nine-millimeter High Powers, and he wore the twin MAC-11s and the rucksack. At the big door they paused, and Natty pulled her quietly into The Ratel's room.

The door opened and a guard walked in, rifle slung over his shoulder. He stopped and stared in horror at the corpse of Pedro, and Natty sent him reeling unconscious into the wall with a roundhouse kick to the side of the head. Tracker ran over and looked out the window and ran back to the room.

"He was too big, there's one coming who's smaller," he whispered to Fancy.

"What are you talking about?" she asked.

"Shh . . ."

A smaller guard walked in the door, and Tracker stepped out spinning, and his right foot swept up in a hook kick that caught the man flush on the jaw, breaking it. Tracker's left-hand reverse punch shattered the man's cheekbone and nose before his limp body had fallen from the kick. Again, he peeked out the door, summoned Fancy over, and started removing the man's uniform.

She helped him and then put the uniform on. She took the man's AK-47, his harness, and stripped the other guard of his extra magazines. She joined Natty at the door where he was looking out into the prison yard. He pulled her to him, kissed her, and held her tightly against his body.

He looked down into her eyes and said softly, "You know, we're going to get awfully bloody before we get out of this country."

"I know, Natty," she said. "If we don't make it, Natty, I want you to know that I love you. If we do make it, I still want you to know it, but I also know that our jobs will keep us apart for a long time."

He smiled softly, "I love you, too, and I agree with you, but even if our careers keep us apart, we can still look forward to vacations."

She smiled broadly, but a tear welled up in her left eye. It ran down her black and blue cheek and dripped onto the collar of the uniform of the Royal Libyan Army.

She said in a tremulous voice, "I want your word

that you'll never tell what happened to me with The Ratel when we get back.''

''You've got my word on one condition.''

''What's that?''

''That you'll get a checkup and go see a good counselor when we get back to the States,'' he said.

''Absolutely,'' she responded. ''I'm not going to let this screw up my life.''

''Good, you ready to go kick some ass, m'lady?'' he asked with a grin.

''Let's do it!''

They both cocked their weapons and ducked out into the darkness. There were four armed guards standing in the archway of the open main gate. Natty grabbed Fancy by the hand and pulled her back inside the door.

He turned to her and said, ''Wait here and keep watch.''

He grabbed the keys and ran to the first floor cell-block area and opened the first door. One by one, he released all the political prisoners who were being held there. They followed him quietly back to the main door where Fancy stood watch.

One of the prisoners grabbed him by the arm and whispered, ''Italiano?''

Tracker said, ''No, American. You speak English?''

''Yes,'' he responded enthusiastically. ''I knew your army would invade someday and save my country.''

Tracker laughed and said, ''Our army hasn't invaded. It's just the two of us.''

The man looked disappointed but quickly regained his enthusiasm and volunteered, ''My name is Sayyid Ibn al-Fasi.''

Tracker said, ''Call me Tracker and her name is Fancy. Tell the men that the gates are open, but there are four armed guards there. Most of the guards are out looking for us. What we'll do is rush the gate in a group and see how many of us can make it.''

Sayyid replied, ''If you don't mind, I have a better idea, I think. Just a minute.''

He spoke in Arabic to several men, and they helped him don the uniform of the first guard whose clothes were too large for Fancy. Several more stripped the uniforms and weapons from other dead soldiers. They followed Sayyid out the door and walked up to the four guards at the gate. Looking out the door, Natty saw several rifles swing and men fall to the ground. He heard a summoning whistle, and he and Fancy ran out to the gate.

''The men and I are going to split up and escape. Where will you go?'' Sayyid asked.

Natty said, ''We have an escape vehicle waiting, but it will only hold two of us.''

15.

Running from the Tiger

THE SQUAD OF guards was exhausted from running through the desert, sand pulling at their weary leg muscles. It was sheer chance that one of the guards tried to lay back on what he thought was a large mound of sand. He fell when the nylon tarp collapsed and landed on the deck of the Hovercopter. The other guards excitedly pulled the tarp off and eagerly inspected the strange craft. The arif, or corporal, with them called his lieutenant and told him. One of the guards looked curiously at the red button labeled BTFOOAI. He pushed it.

Tracker knew what it was when he heard the explosion a mile away in the dunes. He looked at Sayyid and said, "Well, Sayyid, I guess we don't have a vehicle. Can you get us to either Nalut or Nefren?"

Sayyid said, "Yes, I can, but first we must go into Tripoli and hide for several days until they quit searching for us. Muammar al-Qaddafi will be very angry, and many people will suffer who work close to him."

"I understand many of your countrymen don't like

Qaddafi. Is that true?'' Natty asked as the three walked quickly toward Tripoli.

Sayyid laughed and replied, "Many think he is a madman. Only the uneducated has he fooled. Many of the people around him are on our side, but they must be very careful. He is a fanatic, and he is very bad for our country. We need to be close to the United States like Israel is. Look how rich and independent their country is, but many people don't understand this. You must convince your President to invade our country and topple this madman.''

"Our government doesn't often invade other countries, Sayyid,'' Natty said. "Not our usual style. Besides, first we have to get out of Libya alive.''

Just then two military landrovers roared over a sand dune, their headlights falling directly on Natty, Sayyid, and Fancy. Both vehicles immediately moved apart to bear down on the trio. Fancy responded first by swinging her AK-47 up and firing on automatic at the right-hand vehicle. The headlights went out first, as Natty and Sayyid fired at the vehicle on the left. The three looked like old West gunfighters as they stood, legs spread apart, three abreast, firing their weapons at the onrushing steel monsters. Natty's bullets blew out the right front tire on his vehicle at the same time that Fancy's bullets ripped into the left front tire on hers.

The vehicles rammed into each other, bounced off, and careened out of control past the still-shooting trio. Fancy's rolled on its roof and exploded in flames. The other turned over on its side, and soldiers tried to scramble out only to be met by automatic weapons' fire from the three.

Natty led the way as they ran to the unburned landrover. Fancy and Sayyid helped Tracker push the vehicle back onto its wheels. Tracker and Sayyid quickly, without speaking, found the jack and spare and changed the right front tire. They pulled the bodies of the dead guards out and jumped in with Tracker at the wheel. Sayyid reached down and turned on the headlights, but Tracker turned them off immediately.

Frightened, Sayyid said, "We will be killed!"

Fancy laughed and said, "Trust me, Sayyid, he can see without lights."

"But how? Are you a bat? How can you even see *with* the lights while you wear sunglasses?" Sayyid exclaimed.

Barreling down a wide boulevard in the new section of town now, Tracker laughed loudly and replied, "Don't worry, friend, I only wear the sunglasses because I'm totally blind, but I'm really good at guessing."

He careened around a corner, tires squealing loudly and belching smoke. Fancy started laughing with Natty as Sayyid screamed at the top of his lungs.

Out of breath, Sayyid said excitedly, "I have read books about Americans and have seen several movies, but I thought these things only happen in those books and movies. I think maybe all Americans are crazy!"

Natty slid around another corner and started laughing once more with Fancy as Sayyid screamed wildly again. A police cruiser flew out of an alley, siren wailing and lights flashing wildly, as it took off after the three escaped prisoners. Natty rocked the vehicle from side to side as the cops fired at them. Ahead of them, another cruiser swerved into the street and raced at them.

"Hang on!" Natty yelled as he slammed his foot on the brakes and jerked the wheel hard to the left.

Sayyid screamed again, and the landrover slid sideways, tires screaming against the pavement. During the skid, Natty shifted into low, popped the clutch, and stomped on the accelerator. Smoke streamed from the tires as the vehicle now lunged at the police who, seconds before, had been pursuing them.

Natty rested a MAC-11 on the dashboard and fired while Fancy and Sayyid fired through the open windshield. The police car exploded in a whoosh of fire as bullets from behind whipped past their heads.

This time Natty hit the brakes and jerked the wheel hard right and executed another 180-degree powerturn. They took off at the other cruiser and again opened fire. Tracker aimed the vehicle straight at the cruiser that kept coming at them.

Fancy finally stood up on the seat, her head and upper body poking out of the sunroof. She rested her elbows on the roof, the butt of a Browning High Power clutched with both hands.

She yelled at the oncoming Libyan cops, "Time to meet Allah, assholes!"

Aiming carefully at the hood and grill of the car, knowing that the vehicle's speed and momentum would be moving the windshield forward into her line of fire, she squeezed the trigger fifteen times rapid-fire. The fourth bullet took out the driver. The cruiser went into a high-speed spin and crashed sideways through a store window.

Within minutes, five more cruisers were pursuing the three down the broad darkened street. Since it was two hours before dawn, the street was otherwise deserted.

Tracker had no idea where he was going and Sayyid wasn't trying to give directions. The Libyan knew the city like the palm of his hand and figured he'd let Tracker drive wherever he needed to go. If they were lucky enough to elude the police, then he could lead them to a safe haven.

"Uh-oh," Fancy said as she pointed down the street.

There were four police cruisers pulled across the broad boulevard and a phalanx of cops was behind the barrier, their guns drawn.

Natty said, "Quick, buckle your seat belts."

Sayyid put his on, but Fancy first reached across to secure Tracker's before she buckled her own.

Natty squeezed the frames of his glasses and zoomed in on the roadblock still three blocks distant. Then he readjusted the glasses.

Tracker said, "Both of you start firing at the roadblock and hang on."

The boulevard was separated by a pipe fence running down the center and was two lanes wide in each direction with a third curb lane for parking. There were modern stores and apartment buildings on both sides of the street, and there were wide sidewalks with regularly spaced lampposts. Libyan flags hung straight down from horizontal flagpoles sticking out from many of the stores. Compact cars were parked along both sides of the street.

Fancy and Sayyid both started shooting out the windshield and a couple of policemen braved the fire to return it.

When they were two blocks away, Natty suddenly swerved to the right, and the landrover roared onto the sidewalk. The police behind the barricade opened fire as the landrover tore down the walkway, a protective wall of parked cars between it and the cops. A fusillade of bullets shattered storefront windows along the sidewalk as Natty zipped along. He came to a curb and shot across the intersection and went back on the side-walk.

"Natty, they'll get us when we pass by!" Fancy yelled above the firing.

"Just shoot back and keep their heads down!" he hollered back.

With just twenty yards to go, Natty yelled, "Hang on! Grit your teeth and tighten your guts!"

With Sayyid screaming wildly, Natty downshifted, swerved the vehicle hard to the left directly into the back of a parked Volkswagen beetle. As he hit the back of the car, Natty floored the accelerator in second gear, and the landrover sailed up and out, passing over the cruisers and the heads of Libyan police officers.

They hit the street first on the back wheels followed by the front, and Natty had to jerk the wheel left and then right as the landrover violently bounced its way into a proper attitude. The three ducked as they tore down the street with a barrage of angry bullets zipping after them.

Sirens blared as several cops jumped in their cruisers and tried to pull them out of the tight blockade.

Tracker whipped his battered vehicle around the corner, but this time Sayyid was laughing and whooping wildly. Fancy and Tracker both laughed at Sayyid's antics.

Giddy and breathless, Sayyid said, "Tracker, how did you do that? I saw you on the television when I was in Italy. You are not blind; you are the *Six Million Dollar Man*!"

Tracker and Fancy laughed with genuine mirth.

He barreled the vehicle down a narrower street, then all of a sudden the engine sputtered. Natty looked at the gas gauge and saw that it registered empty. He slammed on the brakes and jumped out, pulling Fancy by the hand. Sayyid followed as Natty opened a manhole cover, and they scampered down. He replaced the cover as the first cruiser skidded around the corner.

The sewer was pitch black, and Sayyid said, "Tracker, what do we do now? Do you have matches?"

Natty grabbed Fancy's hand and pulled her without speaking.

They passed by Sayyid in the dark and Natty said, "Grab his hand."

Fancy did so and Tracker led them through the darkness at a trot. It was frightening for both Fancy and Sayyid, but following Natty, they made good time and put a good distance between themselves and the police who were frantically searching buildings. Natty finally slowed the pace slightly after several blocks with no sign of pursuit. Sayyid was very much out of breath.

They finally came to a stop, and Tracker told them to catch their breath. He led Sayyid up a ladder and they cautiously looked out from the manhole.

Sayyid pointed to a large building complex and said, "That is the residence and headquarters of Colonel Qaddafi."

They crawled back down, and Natty pulled something out of his pack and said, "Wait here, I'll be right back."

Fancy said, "Where are you going, Natty?"

She couldn't see him smile in the darkness as he said, "I have to deliver an important message."

Tracker crawled out of the manhole with perhaps another half-hour of darkness left and crawled on his belly to the curb. He saw several sets of guards walking the grounds but none was close to the massive wooden door of the main building. No one looked in his direction.

He concentrated intently on what he was about to do, although it was something he had done countless times since early childhood. He stood and held the curved dagger that had belonged to The Ratel, and his arm went forward in a whipping motion. The dagger sailed through the air as Natty flattened on the street and watched it. It slammed into the massive door with a loud *thwack*.

Natty crawled back through the shadows and went head first into the manhole, hearing the voices of startled guards behind him. He turned himself around at the top of the ladder and quietly slipped the cover into place.

Climbing down, he reached out and took Fancy's hand and led the two off into the darkness. He stopped two blocks away and said, "Sayyid, can you lead us the right way with a flashlight, since you know what's above?"

"Yes, I think so," he replied.

Tracker had Fancy pull a small but powerful flashlight out of his pack and hand it to Sayyid. He led off.

Fancy said, "Natty, what was that about back there?"

Tracker laughed and said, "We were just across from Wacky Qaddafi's headquarters, so I threw The Ratel's knife and stuck it in the door."

Both Fancy and Sayyid laughed as they passed through knee-deep water and sewage.

They heard voices behind them, and Tracker told them to go on quickly. He turned to face the pursuers, and followed Fancy and Sayyid at a distance.

Fancy whispered back as loudly as she dared, "What if we get separated?"

Natty whispered, "Go to the beach. I'll find you."

As they went around one bend, there was a ladder and manhole above. Natty went up the ladder quickly and removed the cover. Sunlight flooded the shaft. They went at top speed through the sewer, trying to get away from the lighted area. They heard the voices of their pursuers behind them.

Out of breath, Fancy turned and murmured to Tracker, "Why did you remove the manhole cover?"

"Slow them down. They probably figured we climbed out there. If they have a big force, they could've sent part of their people. If there's just a handful, they would have all stopped to check."

"You think it will give us enough time to get away?"

"No," he replied. "If they're big, they'll have some people climb out and run ahead of us to set up a blocking force. That's why you two are taking off while I occupy them."

"No!" Fancy said. "If you stay . . ."

Several bursts from automatic weapons cut her speech short. Silhouetted between her and the distant muzzle flashes was the sight of Natty being hit and flung backward by the shots. She heard his body splash into the sewer water. She started to run back, but his voice stopped her. She thought he'd been hit hard in the intestines since he sounded as if the wind had been knocked out of him.

"No!" he commanded. "I'll get killed if I have to worry about you. *Go!*"

She understood and knew enough about this type of situation to know that to argue would be fatal for both. That had been one of the first things Fancy'd learned as an intelligence operative. It was why a good military force can never be a democracy.

She heard a tremendous fight behind her as she and

Sayyid ran full speed down the dank passageway. Sayyid made turns every time his flashlight beam revealed such an option. He knew that was their only chance for escape. After fifteen minutes of running, totally exhausted and sweating bullets, Sayyid and Fancy decided to chance leaving the sewers. He climbed a ladder and lifted the manhole cover. She saw a broad smile cross his lips.

"What is it?" she asked.

He said, "This is my old neighborhood. It is better here. My family has many friends. They will search the place where I was living when I was arrested but maybe not so much here."

They crawled out and walked through the now-crowded alleyway. Several people recognized Sayyid, but the looks they gave him were conspiratorial—a wink here, a nod there.

He turned to Fancy and said, "We will be safe here. There are many of us who are not looked on with favor by the colonel. They will warn us."

"Why were you arrested?" Fancy asked, not really caring but wanting to divert her thoughts from Natty's obvious death.

The firing had been long, hard, and vicious. She could not reasonably fathom how anyone could have lived through such a battle. Fancy, however, like Tracker, was a survivor, and even though the man she loved had died, she had to think first of self-preservation. Later she could mourn Tracker. Fancy knew that Tracker would have felt the same way.

She didn't often think about her early religious instruction, but she did remember a verse from the Bible, in which Jesus was scolding some people, and He'd said: *"Let the dead bury the dead."*

She figured that was very good advice indeed. Her thoughts were interrupted by Sayyid's answer to her question.

"My father was a shrewd and respected merchant," he said. "I got to go to school in England and also spent time in Italy. My father spoke out against Qaddafi and I did the same. Then I joined an underground group. There was an informer—I and others were arrested."

"And your father?" she asked.

"We were told that he was drunk and was killed by a hit-and-run driver, but my father never drank," he replied sadly. "Come. In here, we will be safe."

Sayyid led Fancy into a modest stone house. After Sayyid introduced Fancy to his friend, Ahmad Jalloud, they both fell down exhausted.

A few hours later, Fancy stirred in her sleep as she felt someone cover her with a cloth. Another time, she awakened briefly to hear Ahmad and Sayyid speaking, but the tone of their conversation put her at ease.

When the bullets spurted from the automatic weapons behind Natty, they sent him flying into the dirty water running through the sewer. His first thought was about the bullet wound in his thigh from the Hovercopter battle. He had dressed the wound, and he'd seen that the bullet had passed cleanly through the fleshy part of his thigh. It was sore but had been healing without a problem. Fancy didn't even know about it. But now, contact with the putrid water might cause infection.

The bullets fired in the sewer had struck the heavy steel manhole cover Natty had been carrying as a shield. Worn on the edges, it had fit through the hole. The sheer power of the fusillade had knocked the wind out of him and thrown him to the ground, but the cover had proved effective as he fought the squad of soldiers with his MAC-11s, killing them all.

Instead of trying to find Fancy and Sayyid, Tracker followed the sewers that headed downhill, thinking they would eventually bring him to the sea. He finally came to what appeared to be the city's main sewer since it was much larger and the water was over his head. Natty floated on his back for an hour, letting the water carry him slightly downward.

Voices speaking Arabic brought him over into a slow dog-paddle. Where he was, the sewer was in total darkness, so he had not been seen, but, of course, he could see. It now appeared that somebody had been thinking. Ahead of him were five cops or soldiers in wet suits spread across the width of the sewer. They were holding a rope that had been stretched across the water's surface, and each held a weapon of some sort. Two uniformed police officers with weapons were above the water on a ladder leading to the street.

Natty was thankful for the MAC-11s and their loaded magazines which would act as a weight belt. He was also glad that his pack had plenty of ammo in it for weight and that most of the items were waterproof. He floated as close as possible while he carefully watched the blockers who shone flashlights into the dark sewer. Natty thought he could hear a distant noise that might be the sea, and he decided to add a super-sensitive hearing capability to the SOD when he got home. *If* he got home.

He took a few deep breaths and went underwater in a whale roll, and his powerful legs began to propel him along the sewer's bottom while he pulled at the water with one hand and dragged his pack behind him with the other. His lungs felt like overinflated balloons ready to burst. The brown sewer water was too murky for the OPTIC System to function, so he had to guess.

He pushed himself along, making sure that some part of him always touched the bottom. Lungs still bursting, Tracker let out little bits of air and kept swimming. He finally surfaced slowly. His head broke the surface of the water quietly, and Natty turned and saw the backs of the men, less than eight feet away. He took a quick breath, silently slipped back into the foul-smelling water, and kicked away.

Ten minutes later, Natty was swimming in the Mediterranean. He swam to a nearby pier and went underneath.

That night, under the cover of darkness, Natty climbed out of his perch under the pier and found a hiding place in an adjacent warehouse. The bullet wound in his leg had not opened during his ordeal, so he didn't have to worry so much about infection.

Everyday, wrapped in a *baraccan*, Fancy went to the beach accompanied by either Ahmad or Sayyid. She'd been doing this for two weeks, and there was still no sign of Natty.

Most of the time Fancy stared at the sea and silently grieved for her lover, but there was something inside her that wouldn't accept his death.

Ahmad and Sayyid had treated her well and had been working on an escape for her and Sayyid, who had decided to go to England. They both had to force her to leave the beach to eat meals and sleep.

On the fifteenth day after her separation from Tracker, she was walking along the beachfront with

Sayyid past a ditch that ran down into the water. It had just turned dark, and she had talked Sayyid into waiting a little longer.

A hand came from the ditch, grabbed her ankle, and pulled her into the water. She stifled a scream.

Tracker removed his mouthpiece and gave her a shushing sign. She hugged him tightly and found he was wearing scuba gear.

He whispered to Sayyid, "Sayyid, it's Tracker. Stand there and don't look down. They've been looking all over for me for two weeks now. They've found two hiding places, and I was almost caught stealing food one night. We must say good-bye now, my friend. Do you have somewhere to escape to?"

Sayyid looked straight ahead and whispered, "Yes, I will go to England. You are a lucky man, Tracker; she would not believe that you were dead. She would not give up. May Allah be with you both."

Softly, Fancy whispered, "Thank you, Sayyid, and thank Ahmad for me, too. Good luck."

Tracker said, "You must go now, my friend; they are near. You will be in our memories."

Without speaking, Sayyid walked away, and Tracker held Fancy tightly in the shadows.

She said, "Natty, how did you . . ."

He interrupted, "When they fired at me, I was holding the manhole cover I removed. I killed them all and I wasn't hurt. I've been hiding from them, and I retrieved this rebreathing apparatus and fins from my first infiltration. I'd buried them a few miles from here. Now follow me. We have to go somewhere that's safer. No noise."

He spun around in the water and started swimming quietly toward the sea. Fancy swam next to him.

When they made it to open water, they turned west-ward and paralleled the shoreline. A vehicle came along the beach, and the two dived underwater and kept swimming, buddy-breathing with Tracker's mouth-piece.

After an hour, Natty led Fancy out of the water and up a rope ladder into an old fishing boat. Inside, he lit a lantern.

"Who owns this?" Fancy asked.

"Hell, I don't know," Natty responded. "It looked deserted, so I just moved in."

She laughed and started removing his wet clothes, followed closely by her own. Tracker lay down on the bunk and signaled her to join him. Their lips met as their chilly bodies pressed tightly against each other.

Natty kissed her softly and, trying to control his ir-regular breathing, said, "I love you, Fancy."

"I love you, too," she replied breathlessly. Then they melted into each other.

When they were finished, the two lovers collapsed in each other's arms and lay a long time lightly touching and kissing each other's lips and faces.

Natty finally got up and put on his underwater gear. He turned to her and said, "I'll be back in a few min-utes. I have to go find us some food."

She lay on her back, still nude and as sexy as ever, and smiled at him. Her eyes opened wide and there was a loud crack from a pistol. Tracker saw a large bullet hole appear between her eyes. Her body twitched once and she died. The man in the doorway had a sadistic sneer on his face as he pointed the .45 automatic at Natty's face.

"Amigo," the man started to say, but he was cut off by Natty's lunge punch and loud yell. The punch shattered the assassin's nose and was so powerful he flew backward off the boat and into the water. Tracker followed him out the door, a primal scream escaping his lips, but shots from the dock and the shoreline forced him back. He caught a glimpse of the Latino swimming for shore as soon as he surfaced. But now that Libyan police officers had discovered his location, Natty knew he had to get away.

Tracker had to save himself. He looked at Fancy's body lying lifeless on the bed, and he covered it with an old blanket. Self-preservation had to take precedence over sentiment, and he knew Fancy would have understood that. It was one of the rules of the game they both had played. In that fleeting moment, Natty decided that since he couldn't pursue the assassin now, he'd some day hunt the man down and kill him. He'd memorized every detail about him and was confident of victory in the end. He made another promise to himself then; he wouldn't even think about marriage or any kind of permanent relationship with another woman as long as he was in this business.

He grabbed his pack, pulled out one of the MAC-11s, cocked it, zipped the bag, and put the mouthpiece of the rebreather in his mouth. Clutching his fins and pack in one hand, he moved to the door. Tracker flipped the selector lever on the machine pistol to full automatic and took two steps out the door, firing as he ran, and kept firing as he dived into the water amidst a hail of fire from the Libyans.

Underwater, Natty put the weapon in the pack, swam directly underneath the boat, and remained there. He knew they would soon have the shoreline swarming with frogmen, heat-sensing devices, vessels, searchlights, and perhaps even trained dolphins like those the US

Navy had secretly used in Vietnam to patrol for North
Vietnamese underwater saboteurs.

He listened to the footsteps of cops in the fishing boat
for over an hour. He also heard the engines of boats
cruising the area.

Two hours after the killing, Tracker slipped up the
side of the boat. Fancy's body was still there, but now
it was inside a black plastic body bag, and it was
guarded by a lone police officer.

Tracker walked down the hatchway and straight to
the astonished cop. Not a word was said; Natty side-
kicked the cop at the base of the jaw and heard the
neck break with a loud snap. The cop fell dead in a
limp pile.

Tracker got Fancy's pistols and strapped on the holsters after removing the rebreather. He took the cop's
gun and put it into his waistband, and he pulled his
camouflage jumpsuit out of his pack and put it on. He
decided to leave the MAC-11s in the pack until he had
a chance to clean and dry them.

He lightly touched the stiffening body in the black
plastic bag and went up the steps wearing the cop's hat.
He walked off the end of the dock within sight of several cops and as many soldiers, all engaged in various
activities. To them, he was just the silhouette of a tall
cop.

Tracker walked to the nearest police cruiser, climbed
in, started it, and drove away slowly. He looked in the
rearview mirror as he pulled away and saw a flash a
millisecond before he heard a bullet slam into the trunk
of the car. Tracker floored it and headed southeast along
the ocean. His was the only cruiser close to the dock,
so he knew he had something of a jump on them, but
they finally appeared, a sea of flashing lights, in his

rearview. Natty prayed for no helicopters, at least for now.

He turned due south and roared through the city. He saw signs indicating he was on his way toward the airport, and he considered trying to go directly there and steal a plane or helicopter but then decided against it. He barreled down a boulevard and saw that the cars behind him were not gaining much.

The police kept after him and could see his tail lights far ahead. The sergeant in the closest cruiser behind him called in and gave his location, speed, and direction. Preparations were made to set up several different roadblocks, including one with Soviet-made tanks. A pair of assault helicopters was warming up at Wheelus Airfield.

The road ahead made a sharp turn to the right, and the sergeant hoped the American wouldn't turn off while he was out of sight. The sergeant was soon rounding the same turn only to see Natty's car go airborne at the next bend. It exploded in a ball of flame in midair, flipped over twice, and came crashing down on its top.

Thirty seconds later, his cruiser and the others behind him skidded to a stop at the crash site. They couldn't get close to the tongues of flame licking up into the night sky.

If they had looked for it, they would have seen a rubber hose sticking out of the sand on the other side of the road one hundred yards back from the site of the wreckage. It had been cut from the rebreathing apparatus now inside the burning car. The end of the hose in the soft sand was still attached to the mouthpiece that was now inside Natty's mouth as he lay on his back, firmly pinching his nostrils.

Natty had made up his mind to survive. He also

hoped his next assignment would place him in a country with more hiding places, so he wouldn't have to bury himself in hot, itchy sand.

Tracker reached down, pulled a kerchief out of a pocket, inched it up, and plugged his nostrils with it. Using the powers of concentration he'd learned in the martial arts and the patience he'd acquired from his grandfather, Tracker lay in the sand, unmoving, for three hours. He then dug his way out and crawled on his belly for another hour and took refuge in a small wooden shed used to store dates.

The following day, a Soviet-made 2,000-kilo truck pulled in and workers started loading dates. The task took several hours, but the truck finally pulled away from the shed and headed south toward the airport. When it pulled away no one saw the man who hung underneath, hands and feet astraddle the axle.

Tracker managed to hold on until the truck pulled into the cargo loading area at Tripoli International Airport. He dropped off and hid among some large crates.

Natty had to figure out a way to make it out to the wastelands to his specially built F-15E Eagle and get out of Libya, or he would have to find another way out and blow the jet up. The F-15E Eagle was the newest prototype of the F-15 Eagles. It was introduced to the US Air Force in 1988, but as yet was still not available for general use since the F-15Cs and F-15Ds currently in operation still had plenty of life. It was unthinkable to let one of America's most sophisticated warplanes fall into the hands of Qaddafi Duck.

He studied the airport all day, but his eyes kept coming back to two C-47s with the identifying markings of the 300-aircraft-strong Libyan air force. Natty knew the Libyans had acquired nine C-47 twin-propeller cargo planes from the US when relations were normal in the days of King Idris. He also knew that the US had put a freeze on weapons, aircraft, and parts going to Libya in 1975 since Qaddafi supported the PLO and other terrorist organizations. Libya had then become the Soviet Union's second largest arms customer in Africa, just behind Ethiopia. Because of this, Tracker figured the two C-47s must be among the few C-47s still flying.

He tried to imagine why those two military aircraft were sitting there and where they might be headed. They were prop-driven aircraft, so they probably weren't going a long distance. There were several major air bases near Tobruk and Benghazi and several more to the south. The main military air base near Tripoli was the large Uqba ben Nafi Air Base, but these planes were here at the commercial airport.

Natty reasoned that some import or delivery was coming in from somewhere and part of it was going to the military and part to the civilian populace. Boxes of supplies were loaded onto the aircraft and then a bus came over from the main airport terminal. A number of men disembarked and boarded the lead plane. Several wore the uniforms of Cuba, and they were conversing with the rest who were in civilian clothing.

That was it then, he thought; Cuban military and probably intelligence advisors had flown into Libya on commercial aircraft and were being taken by military aircraft to an installation. Canvas mailbags were loaded onto the second plane. Tracker now had his answers. There was a Libyan army unit on maneuvers somewhere in the desert and the two planes were being used to resupply them. The planes had been sent to pick up imported supplies and the passengers at the same time to simplify logistics.

But where were they going? The Mediterranean was directly to the north so that direction was certainly out of the question. Less than one hundred miles to the west was Tunisia, and there was a major road network in that direction, so trucks and buses would have been easier and less expensive. The same held true to the east. Tracker concluded that the two planes were headed somewhere south, and that was where he wanted to go.

He started formulating a plan.

Thirty minutes later, an airport worker lay unconscious under a truckload of ground nuts, and Natty was thinking about how uncomfortable it was to wear a scarf around one's head and face. Natty picked up different objects and carried them, as if working, and slowly over the next half-hour made his way two hundred yards to the nearest hangar. A large structure, it was strewn with single- and twin-engine aircraft, both within its confines and out on the adjoining tarmac.

Tracker was questioned twice by Libyans who may have merely been asking the time of day. One was now dead in the cargo compartment of an old Piper, and the other was very comatose in a maintenance closet.

The aircraft in the hangar, out of the sun, seemed to be the more expensive and newer ones. He checked each plane and finally found what he wanted. He climbed in and pulled out a parachute from behind the pilot's seat. Natty looked it over and it seemed to be packed correctly.

He worked his way back to where he'd hidden his pack and also hid the chute. Natty then went hunting again and soon found what he was looking for, a man wearing a *baraccan*.

Ten minutes passed and Tracker stepped out from the cargo area wearing the bulky garment over the parachute. Acting important and carrying a clipboard and pencil, he walked directly to the second C-47 and pretended to check things off.

He noticed an airport worker out of the corner of his eye. The man was watching Natty with a look a suspicion. Tracker walked to the left front of the plane and gave the landing gear a mock inspection. He then looked up at the pilot and gave him the thumbs up sign, and the pilot responded with a wave and a nod.

After what seemed to Tracker like an eternity, the planes finally cranked up and got ready for take-off, but not before some of the Cuban advisors decided to ride in Natty's aircraft. He had planned to dispatch the one or two crew members in the cargo part of the plane, hope not to be discovered, and jump out if it went anywhere close to his jet.

The scenario changed now. He had to come up with a new plan. He didn't want to shoot it out with fifteen Cuban soldiers. Besides, he had buried the MAC-11s near his hideout in the cargo area after pouring acid on the trigger mechanisms. He had also transferred as many small items as possible to his pockets and buried the rest of his pack. It was too bulky to conceal. He carried the two Browning's and had tucked one into his boot and the other into his waistband.

The cargo door on the aircraft started closing, and he saw his hopes dimming as he returned a phony wave to one of the onboard Cubans. The door closed completely, and the same worker who had eyed him with suspicion turned and looked directly at him, so Tracker ran over and removed the right wheel chock and got a wave from the man who had just removed the other one. The ground crew dispersed and headed toward the tower, and Natty made a decision.

He ran after the now-taxiing plane and dived onto the tail section. He stripped away the *baraccan* and clung to the right tail strut. The big tail section protected him from observation from the terminal as the plane followed its twin out to the end of the runway. Once there, he crawled over and straddled the large tail upright. The two planes checked flaps, waited a few minutes for tower instructions, and turned around to take off left to right from the tower's view. Natty lay flat on the left tail section now and held on for dear life.

The veteran aircraft bitched and howled all the way down the runway, but it lifted off and sailed into the blue.

The climb was the hardest part for Natty. It took every ounce of his strength to cling to the plane while gravitational forces and prop turbulence tried their best to rip him from his perch. Once away from the airport, Natty again straddled the big tail upright, and it was somewhat easier to hang on since it supported him to some extent.

Inside, the pilot was bitching about the unusual turbulence.

The wind tried to tear him from the plane every second, but Tracker managed to stay with it. He was elated as he saw Azizia pass beneath him and then Gharian, Tigrinnia, and Assaba. They were headed southeast on a course directly toward his jet.

Fifteen minutes later, Natty reckoned they were close to the jet. He looked at a device he had strapped onto his left wrist above the Tracker System. He pushed a button and it beeped and displayed an arrow pointing toward the waiting jet. It was seven kilometers due west. Natty saw a long column of tanks near a cluster of tents on the southern horizon, so he knew he'd be spotted on take-off, but he couldn't worry about that now.

Tracker jumped up and away from the tail section and started falling through the blast furnace-like air. He used his hands to stabilize himself in a proper free-fall attitude and watched the horizon. He avoided looking straight down since he wanted to avoid what jumpers refer to as "ground rush," when the ground, all of a sudden, seems to rush up. Natty knew of more than one skydiver who'd panicked and frozen as a result of ground rush, and now he wasn't even wearing an altimeter to assure him he had sufficient time to open his chute.

When he estimated he was about one thousand feet above the desert floor, Natty pulled the ripcord and said a quick prayer.

He felt a jerk as the parachute opened. Tracker reached above each shoulder and grabbed the nylon risers, his eyes following the suspension lines up to where they attached to the canopy. None of them were across the canopy, and it was fully inflated. Natty breathed a sigh of relief. The canopy was an old T-10 parachute that was last used by the US Army in the late sixties.

He didn't notice any discernible wind, so he just enjoyed the ride to the ground.

Not wanting to take a chance on a stand-up landing, Tracker hit the ground with a good parachute landing fall. Coming in with a slight forward movement, he hit the ground first with the balls of his feet, legs together and slightly bent. His body partially relaxed, he twisted slightly to the right and next hit on his right calf, thigh, buttock, back, and shoulder. He rolled over in a semi-somersault and came up on his feet. Tracker pulled the lines on one side of the chute, spilling the air from the ground breeze from it and collapsing the canopy. He then gathered it in and S-rolled the lines and chute over his outstretched arms and threw it on the ground, kicking sand over it. Natty then took off at a fast walk toward his jet.

He chewed gum to keep his saliva flowing, alternated between jogging and walking, and made it to the jet in a few hours' time. Once there, he disarmed the self-destruct mechanism and immediately went for the five gallon water tank he had stored in the cockpit. The water was hot, but Natty didn't care. He downed two salt tablets, lots of water, and gorged on food from emergency supplies in the jet.

Natty looked northwest toward Tripoli and pictured Fancy's body, still in its zippered plastic prison. He pictured it as a cocoon from which her soul could never escape. Several tears spilled down his cheeks. He wiped them away, cleared his throat, and looked around unconsciously to ensure no one saw him being a human. Then Natty prepared for take-off.

He was able to take off and disappear over the horizon without being spotted by the army unit since a slight wind kicked up enough sand and dust to obscure the billowing cloud the jet produced. Tracker flew north and held the jet close to the deck until the armored unit was miles behind him. He streaked across the Libyan wastelands, the Gebel Nefusah passing below his thunderous craft. Natty secretly wished he'd be discovered and the Libyans would send their modern MIG-25s after him.

He stayed below radar until he was very close to Tripoli, where he could more easily lose himself amid the heavy air traffic around the capitol. There he went up to the eagles, into the bright sunlight reflecting off the cool blue Mediterranean beneath him.

By now, they knew he wasn't a friendly, but Natty didn't care. He swooped down in a dive at the city of Tripoli directly below him. The sonic boom made those on the ground think they were being attacked again by US fighter-bombers.

He leveled off and turned east along the sea. Natty was sure that Fancy's body had long since been removed, but when he approached the dock mooring the boat on which they'd made love and where she'd been killed, he dropped two napalm cannisters.

The boat did, however, still hold her body and a police guard, left there as bait to attract Natty after they'd checked the charred remains of the cruiser and found no sign of the American.

He was miles away, streaking across the blue sea before anybody called in a report of his air strike. In fact, Tracker was fifty miles beyond Qaddafi's so-called "line of death" before four MIG-25 Foxbats reached the coast. They made a show of flying out over the sea but aborted the mission before chancing an encounter with any American jet drivers. The Libyan pilots had been whacked in the head with a two-by-four enough times by American pilots.

16.

Unfinished Business

WALLY RAMPART SAT with his feet up on his desk while Natty Tracker gave a complete report on his activities. He was, of course, saddened by the death of Fancy Bird, but elated about the elimination of The Ratel and the strong message Natty's mission left with Muammar al-Qaddafi.

The following day found Tracker at FBI headquarters giving a detailed description of Fancy's assassin, and he received a computer-drawn composite of the killer. Showing it around prompted a DEA official to show Natty photographs of a Cuban professional assassin who had been working for the Medellin drug cartel, handling their more important hits. Tracker definitely identified the man. His name was Miguel Atencio. Natty was given the files on him, along with videotapes and photographs. One of the more current photos showed him with a broad smile and his beefy right arm around the narrow shoulders of Dr. Edmund Tetrau.

The next day, Tracker relaxed, played tennis, and went swimming with a much stockier, more tanned, and healthier-looking Peter "Rabbit" Roberts.

The following morning, Natty hopped in his F-15E and headed for Colorado Springs. He parked it in his designated guarded hangar at Petersen Air Force Base and climbed in a silver and black 1976 Corvette Indy Pace Car and headed for the Broadmoor area. As he turned down his street and saw his home, his shoulders sagged with complete relaxation. Two houses down from his, he saw Yuri, the head Soviet spy watching him, coming from the house. Natty chuckled at the thought of the Soviets considering him so important that they had to buy a home near his to keep him under surveillance.

Yuri waved Tracker down. Natty was suspicious, but he pulled over to the curb as the large KGB agent walked over. Natty gave a reassuring pat to the Inter-arms Virginia Dragoon .44 magnum pistol resting comfortably in the holster under his left arm. He watched Yuri's eyes and hands for any untoward movements.

The big Russian leaned into the window and said, "Tracker it iss against all rules to even speak with you."

Tracker nodded and said, "I know," very puzzled by the spy's statement.

The Russian continued, "I have never before spoke with enemy like dis." He paused and cleared his throat.

Tracker chuckled, "I understand. Go ahead."

Yuri said, "I vant tell you that I very sorry about what happened to Doctor Bird."

Tracker was astounded. Perhaps détente was indeed a possibility. Natty believed you should always be willing to shake hands with an enemy as long as your other hand firmly grips a weapon with the index finger curled comfortably around the trigger.

He couldn't think of any ulterior motive the Russian might have in making such a statement.

He finally responded, "Thank you, but why did you tell me that? You could get in quite a bit of trouble, I imagine, by just talking to me."

"Nyet," he said proudly. "Like you, I am hero. That is why I tell you. I know about you much. You and me are much the same but born in different land."

Natty stuck out his hand as he thought about the statement, and it was gripped by the Russian's powerful handshake.

Tracker said, "What's your name?"

The Soviet immediately stiffened and said brusquely, "Does not matter. I must go."

Tracker watched the big man walk up the porch steps and into the house. He heard several angry male voices from within arguing in Russian as he pulled away from the curb and drove to his house.

Tracker spent several days at his house making plans for Edmund Tetrau. He called Wally Rampart and had a conference call with the director of the DEA. He asked for word to be put out by their undercover agents that a certain millionaire industrialist named William H. Rector was struggling to recoup tremendous business losses and had decided to peddle some coke. He had them concoct a convincing cover story that would make a drug merchant drool. The DEA director said their DF readings showed Tetrau to be in San Diego, and he assured Natty that the story would be circulated in all the areas where Tetrau had contacts.

With phony ID's and credit cards sent by overnight courier, Natty flew to Las Vegas, where the commanding general of Nellis Air Force Base had been instructed to keep Natty's jet undercover and under guard.

Tracker took up residence at the Alladin Hotel and Casino. He got a suite that looked down on the casino roof courtyard where there were four tennis courts, a pro shop, and a swimming pool.

Tracker spent his time reading and at night he often looked out the window at the Aladdin's big sign with a scantily clad buxom beauty advertising the famous Abracadabra Show. Looking at the woman in her harem outfit made him think of Fancy and the last time they had made love. Tetrau was indeed going to pay.

After three days, he got a call from Wally; Tetrau was on a jet and apparently headed to Vegas.

The next day he got a call in his room. It was Tetrau, who was staying at the Gold Coast. Natty had put a device on the phone that electronically altered his voice slightly so it would not betray him.

Tracker played it cautiously, as did Tetrau. Edmund carefully felt his way through the conversation, but Natty was convincing. They set up an appointment for eight o'clock that evening. At Tracker's insistence, they would meet at his suite. Tetrau didn't like it, but he was hooked.

At eight o'clock sharp, Tetrau knocked on Tracker's door. The blood drained from Edmund's face as he stared into the muzzle of an Uzi in the hands of Nathaniel Hawthorne Tracker.

Natty said, "Why, Doctor, what an unexpected surprise. Please do come in. Allow me to introduce myself: My name is William H. Rector, down-on-his-luck industrialist."

Edmund couldn't speak.

Tracker spoke softly, "You put Miguel Atencio on me, didn't you?"

"No, Tracker, I swear I didn't!"

"Wrong answer," Natty said. "Can't you for once in your miserable life have the balls to own up to what you've done?"

Natty continued, "You know that Miguel murdered the woman I loved?"

Tetrau couldn't speak; he just cried heavily and whimpered. Tracker shoved the muzzle of the Uzi into his nostril.

Natty said, "Tetrau, take off your trousers."

Edmund shook his head and pleaded, "Please, Tracker, no."

Tracker shoved the barrel of the gun a little harder, and Edmund removed his pants. Tracker walked him over to the dresser, reached in while holding the Uzi to Tetrau's nose with his other hand, and handed Tetrau an athletic supporter with an explosive attached to the cup.

The weasel shook as Natty nudged him, but he put the jock strap on over his underwear and got back into his trousers. Natty backed up, pulled a small black box out of his pocket, and pulled the antenna out. Natty put his finger on the detonator button.

Tracker smiled broadly, "We're going to leave now, Eddie. That's an explosive device on that jock that'll *really* get your nuts off if I push this button. Now we're going downstairs and through the casino, and I'll have my finger on the detonator. If you even fart, I'll not only de-ball you, but de-leg you as well. Understand?"

Tetrau screwed up his courage and said, "If you push that button, you'll get killed, too, Tracker."

Natty just grinned and held up his left ring finger and unscrewed it, removed the cylinder, and showed Tetrau the stump.

He said, "Tetrau, you're partly responsible for this.

More importantly, you're directly responsible for the death of a beautiful young woman I loved very deeply. Now, you know my background and reputation. Do you think I'd even hesitate for a second to blow your crotch off if you so much as smile wrong?''

Tetrau looked at Tracker a moment and replied, ''No.''

''Let's go, '' Natty commanded, setting the Uzi on the dresser and sticking the detonator in his pocket.

They rode down the elevator and walked out the front of the casino. Natty handed his parking stub to a valet, and the man arrived a few minutes later with Natty's rented Cadillac. Tracker slipped a five dollar bill into the man's hand as the door was held open for him.

The car's interior was sweltering, but it cooled off by the time Natty reached West Charleston Boulevard. He headed west and soon saw that he was being followed.

They kept going west toward Red Rocks, a popular getaway spot for Las Vegas residents. Tetrau was drenched with sweat, which only made his shaking worse in the now-chilly air conditioning. Outside of town, Natty pulled off on a dirt road and then off that at a small wash. The other car pulled up quickly behind him. Four monstrous-looking Columbians got out. They all pulled guns and walked forward.

Tracker pulled the detonator out of his pocket, held it up, and said, ''No-no, amigos. If I push this button, old Doctor Tetrau here is going to shit his pants in a very big way. Even if you shoot me, I'll still push the button, and your job is to protect him.''

The apparent leader of the bodyguards said, ''Doctore, comb heere.''

Edmund started walking toward them but stopped

when Natty said, "Hold it, Doc. You know how much I'd hate to split your britches."

The leader again said, "Comb heere, doctore." Then he aimed at Tracker and said, "I can turn heem off like a ligh bulb."

"Maybe you're right," Natty said, raising his hands and grinning like a little boy caught with his hands in the cookie jar.

Tetrau, relieved, walked quickly to the bodyguards, and Natty made his move. He dived to his left, and the leader's bullet split the air where Tracker's head had been. Natty slapped his pocket and that activated the detonator. Dr. Edmund Tetrau was torn in three pieces by the explosion.

The bodyguard leader fell with a large jagged piece of Tetrau's hipbone stuck in his forehead. The others were all on the ground, covered with bits of flesh, blood, and intestines.

One picked up his Uzi to fire, and Natty's hand came up from his ankle where a small holster now showed. In his hand was a lightweight Glock Model 19 nine millimeter automatic. The deadly little weapon with its sawed-off barrel spouted flames as Natty's first four shots blasted into the man's shirt pocket in a tight cluster. A bullet stung Natty's cheek, and he dived right and, rolling, fired and hit the shooter with six shots to the chest.

Natty was now in a prone position resting on both elbows, and the Glock was aimed at the chest of the last man. The man stared at Tracker and dropped his .45 automatic and raised his hands. Natty pictured his favorite aunt who cried whenever she tried to talk about her cocaine addicted twin daughters. He unloaded the rest of the eighteen-round magazine into the body-guard.

Natty heard sirens in the distance and saw flashing lights coming up Charleston. He got into the Cadillac and pulled away with his lights off. He sped off toward the approaching cruisers, still a mile away, and turned left on the first road he came to, turned right on the next, and drove toward town. He could still hear the sirens in the distance to his right rear now. He hit Rainbow Boulevard, turned right, and then went left on Charleston. He was home free.

He waited several days before he checked out of the hotel, and he even managed to win one hundred and thirty dollars on a draw poker slot machine.

A week after Natty returned home, he was summoned to NORAD. He went into a highly polished conference room, spit-shined AP's guarding the door, and saw before him Wally Rampart, the Secretaries of Defense and State, the directors of the FBI, CIA, DIA, DEA, and the President of the United States. Tracker sat down, and the President spoke:

"Mr. Tracker, you've proven yourself a true patriot and a vital asset to this nation. In case you don't know, Colonel Qaddafi has put a bounty on your head of fifty million dinars which I believe at the current rate of exchange, is about ten million dollars."

The President thought about this a minute, chuckled, and continued, "I think you made him angry."

Everyone laughed.

The President went on, "If it were possible, I'd have a major press conference, present you to the public, and award you the Medal of Freedom, but I don't think either of us wants that. I do want to express our sincere respect and gratitude and offer my pledge to grant you whatever you need in your fight against our enemies. Is there anything that you want, Mr. Tracker?''

Natty thought a minute and stood. All eyes were focused on him.

He replied, ''Yes, there is, Mr. President.''

The Chief Executive clapped his hands and said, ''Good. I don't care what it is. If we don't have it, we'll get it for you. What is it?''

Natty grinned and said, ''An assassin named Miguel Atencio.''